The house had the sullen, hollow feeling of abandonment. Even the furniture was gone. I collapsed breathless on the floor. The boards were soggy and rotten. My pants soaked through when I sat down. I didn't bother to get up. I couldn't. I didn't care.

"Ronny —" I started.

"Quiet. They're less than a mile away. They'll hear you."

He was right about that, too.

The dead were coming. They were coming for me.

Bayou Dogs

Look for these titles in
THE HAUNTING OF DEREK STONE series:

#1: City of the Dead

#2: Bayou Dogs

#3: The Red House

#4: The Ghost Road

Bayou Dogs

Tony Abbott

Scholastic Inc.

NEW YORK TORONTO LONDON AUCKLAND SYDNEY
MEXICO CITY NEW DELHI HONG KONG BUENOS AIRES

ISBN-13: 978-0-545-03430-2
ISBN-10: 0-545-03430-2

12 11 10 9 8 7 6 5 4 3 2 1 9 10 11 12 13 14/0

Printed in the U.S.A. 40

First printing, March 2009

To Those We See Again

CONTENTS

Bayou Dogs

ONE

Speeding Up

The night streets slithered in front of us like dark snakes. They urged us every wrong way, crisscrossed one another, coiled back on themselves, stopped abruptly.

My brother Ronny wasn't having any of it. He kept running straight, feet slapping the wet pavement. His hand gripped mine, dragging me forward.

Like madmen fleeing their shadows, my mind told me, *or the shadows of others.*

Like so many times before, I had no time to wonder where those words came from. I just ran past houses, shops, restaurants, through crowded alleys — the whole noisy mess of the French Quarter at night.

My footsteps pounded the ground, jarred my bones. I tried to dodge the puddles as I ran. No luck. I barreled on and hoped I wouldn't fall on my face. I couldn't slow down. I couldn't rest. I couldn't stop.

"This way," Ronny said. "Hurry up!"

"I'm hurrying," I said, gasping for air.

"Not fast enough!" he snarled. "They're gaining on us."

I already knew that.

We'd been racing through the streets for over an hour in the middle of the night. We still couldn't shake them. No matter where we ran, the low voices pierced my ear, whispering, hissing, growling a mile behind us, half a mile, getting closer. Horrible voices.

Their voices.

They used to be people, but they weren't people anymore.

They were the dead. And now they were back.

The shadows of others, my mind said again. I shook my head. There were a lot of things I didn't understand rattling around up there.

"Behind us and to our left," Ronny said. "Five minutes at most. I hear them calling each other."

I nodded. "So do I —"

"Well, thanks to you, we can't outrun them," he snapped, throwing down my hand. "We have to hide. Follow me."

Ronny was angry, but he was right. I was out of shape. I did slow us down.

He turned abruptly and entered a side street. It was darker there. Two of the three streetlamps were out. The third flickered. Ronny scanned the houses on both sides of the street, looking for a vacant one. I watched his eyes dart back and forth, grateful for the chance to stop running. My lungs burned, my throat ached, my knees quaked under me.

I was fat. I was scared. Life was speeding up. Everything around me was spinning. I hated it. School, friends, family, home — everything I knew — was gone.

"Keep it down a little," Ronny said. "You're moaning again."

Maybe I was. You'd be moaning, too, if you were in my shoes. You might be, soon enough.

Ronny turned his head slowly from side to side, then twitched. He took a short step toward one dark house, paused, took another step.

"That one's empty," he whispered. "Come on . . ."

He loped down the narrow side yard and up a set of wooden steps. He forced open the back door with a quick thrust of his arm. There was a splintering crack.

Ronny grabbed the door to stifle the noise.

"In," he said.

Stale air, thick with the odor of mold, breathed out at me from the opening. It felt like the house was gasping its last.

"It stinks," I said.

"Cover your nose," he hissed. "Do you want them to find you?" Pushing me inside, he looked out at the street one last time and quickly shut the door behind us.

Ronny was right about the house being empty. It had the sullen, hollow feeling of abandonment. Even the furniture was gone. I collapsed breathless on the floor. The boards were soggy and rotten. Rain had poured in through a busted window and puddled on the floor. My pants soaked through when I sat down. I didn't bother to get up. I couldn't. I didn't care.

"Ronny —" I started.

"Quiet. They're less than a mile away. They'll hear you."

He was right about that, too.

The dead were coming. They were coming for me.

TWO

The Hard Way

My name is Derek Stone. I'm fourteen. And I'll try to make it as simple as possible for you to understand. The dead have come back.

Impossible, right?

Yeah, I wish. If you want the short version, it began a few weeks ago when a train carrying my brother, my father, and me crashed into a steep ravine called Bordelon Gap. Nine passengers were killed. I was lucky. I survived.

Ronny wasn't so lucky. He died.

Sort of.

It's complicated.

I'd found out the hard way about a thing called *translation*. My term. At the very moment of death, when a soul flees its dying body, another soul — one that's been dead for a long time — can take its place and reanimate that body.

How do I know? I know.

First, there are rules I've learned about translation. And no, I didn't make them up. That's something you need to know about me. I don't make things up. Ever.

To begin with, translation can only occur when both people died in identical ways. That's how it was with Ronny. A train had crashed at Bordelon Gap way back in 1938. It was a prison train, carrying a crew of nasty convicts. Because the convicts died just like the victims of my crash, some of them were able to translate into the bodies of the new victims. Ronny's body was taken over by a young prison guard named Virgil Black, who died in that first wreck. Strangely, some bits of my brother were left in him, glimpses of the brother I grew up with, which is why I still call him Ronny.

But with each day, there is less and less of Ronny . . . never mind that now. You'll see.

Back to business. Translation can only happen because of the *Rift* — not my term. I had dug around in old books, searched the Internet, scoured dusty archives, met a handful of strange people, and it all came down to this: The worlds of the living and the dead are separated by a thin, nearly impenetrable fabric. The living — people like you and me — stay on our side. The dead stay on their side.

At least they did.

Sometime in the recent past, the fabric separating the two worlds was ripped. The tear allowed dead souls to slip across and invade dying bodies. Virgil says they've wanted to do that for a long time. Bordelon Gap is — you guessed it — on the Rift.

You don't believe souls can come back from the dead?

Believe it. The road to the afterlife is a two-way street.

Finally, and this is the worst part, the dead are coming back because of the war.

The War.

Ronny jerked away from the window and walked from room to room, obviously searching for something. I was about to ask him what, when he came back with a beat-up broom in his hands.

"Going to clean up?" I asked.

Ronny snapped the long handle over his knee and tossed away the bristled half. Then he swung the three-foot, jagged-tipped stake in the air. "I'll clean up. If I'm lucky."

He scowled and took his position at the front window again. When he did things like this, I wasn't talking to my brother. I was talking to the country boy who had become a fighter in the War.

Virgil remembered bits and pieces about his seventy years in the land of the dead. He told me about a conflict between good and evil that has gone on for centuries. And guess what? Things weren't going so well for the good guys. They were completely outnumbered by dark souls who wanted to annihilate them.

The land of the dead?

I couldn't help imagining vast crumbling cities, teeming with souls twisted by their own evil. And then one day, a spark, a rebellion, a war. From that moment on, there was no going back. The evil fought the decent dead — souls like Virgil, who tried to stop them — and century upon century passed . . . until the fabric tore and the Rift opened. The dead saw their chance to reinhabit the world they left behind, to spread the War among the living.

So they came back.

One of dead who returned is a man named Erskine Cane. Remember that name. Erskine Cane was an arsonist on his way to be executed when the train carrying him and other convicts crashed at the exact place my train did. His twisted soul returned in the body of a young soldier with a crew cut and muscles from here to Houston.

Another convict entered the body of a second soldier, a short, wiry-limbed guy with a weird nervous tic. I called him Twitchy. The conductor from my train was back now, too, though he'd lost an arm in the crash. A gray-haired man I'd fought in the Quarter was another passenger from my train now inhabited by a dark soul. And Cane's mad wife, the only woman in the group, was also in a passenger's body. There were three others out there somewhere — I had seen only their shadows so far — all in bodies of the victims of my crash.

I know. I don't want to believe it, either.

"Why are they taking so long?" Ronny wondered aloud, moving from window to window.

I checked my watch. We'd been running and hiding for nearly two hours already, but as close as the dead sounded at times, they weren't on top of us. The voices closed in, coiled off, then came in again. It sounded like they were circling away and back like waves in a tide. It gave me time to think about how lucky I am.

No, really.

I'm lucky. Virgil Black is one of the good guys. Before he died in the first wreck, besides being a farm-fresh country kid, he had saved the life of a little boy. That boy grew up to be Bob Lemon, now an old musician who had joined our fight against the dead.

All Virgil Black really wanted was to be dead and at peace — but there was no peace, here or there since the War escalated, and he didn't know how to get back there anyway. So he stayed.

I like to think that he stayed to help me. Although right now he was being a snot about my weight.

"Hey, Chubs, how far is Bayou Malpierre?"

Oh, right. There's that, too.

"Five, six hours," I told him. "That bayou's hard to get to."

"Of course," Ronny said. "Everything else is hard. Why not that?"

As if I wasn't dealing with enough weirdness already, Bayou Malpierre was where I nearly drowned when I was four years old.

We had to go there now because — get this — my dad, who everyone believed had died in the train crash, suddenly showed up and told me and Ronny to go to Malpierre and wait for him.

What? After everything else, you think *that's* weird?

Ten years ago, Bayou Malpierre had been all darkness and rain. I was lost in the swamps. I was afraid. Dogs were coming. And I fell into the water. I tried to claw my way to the surface. Water poured into my nose, my ears. My lungs wanted to burst open —

"You're moaning again," said Ronny, his eyes flashing at me now.

"Sorry," I said.

"Just keep it down."

No one knew who had saved my life that night. Not my father, not Ronny, not my mother — I hadn't seen her for the ten years since the bayou incident, anyway. But being in the water so long had damaged my left ear — the ear that could now hear the voices of the dead.

Told you it was complicated.

Ronny parted the curtains carefully and looked out. I did, too. The only streetlamp with a glimmer of life shone dull brown and then sick yellow on the glazed pavement.

Guttering like a failing candle flame, I told myself.

I was really getting annoyed with these random words that kept popping into my mind. I shook my head and focused on the street. Nothing. Not yet.

"Do you think we should move on?" I whispered.

"To where? To your house?" Ronny said. "Think about it."

I felt like saying, "You start," but kept my mouth shut. Since he died, Ronny had no sense of humor.

But he was right about my house. Erskine Cane had torched it just hours before. Why, I'm not sure. But Cane was after me. I knew that.

"Ronny," I started, "about Cane —"

All of a sudden, my cell phone rang.

"Turn that thing off!" Ronny snapped.

"Sorry," I said.

I opened the phone and noticed that I had only two battery bars left. It was Uncle Carl calling. He had been living with us since the crash. He'd been in Oregon on a business trip when our house burned down, but he'd now just now heard about the fire. He was crazy with worry.

"The alarm company finally tracked me down!" Carl yelled in my ear. "There was a break-in at the house? Then a fire? Are you boys okay? What's going on?"

A break-in? I didn't know that part. I lied and told Carl that we were spending the night at my friend Tooley's house. Ronny and I would be meeting with the fire marshal in the morning. I lied and lied. I didn't know exactly what we were doing, but I knew we couldn't stay put. Carl was smart, but easy to fool. He trusted me. I felt like a criminal.

Right. Me, a criminal. Chubby boy, Derek Stone. Me, running for my life from dead people. *I'm* the criminal!

"So you're both all right?" Carl asked, clearly relieved. I told him we were. "I'm coming right home, anyway," he said. "I'll be back there later today."

"We'll see you tonight at Tooley's house," I lied. I had no idea where we'd be tonight. If we'd be anywhere at all.

Carl said he would let the police know that we

were fine. We hung up, and I tucked my phone in my pocket.

"Try to keep that off until we need it," said Ronny, stalking quietly from window to window as if he'd done this sort of thing before. Watching him reminded me of his fight with Cane at Bordelon Gap. I thought of Cane's equally twisted wife again. From what I knew, she was now in the body of the mother of a girl who had been on the train with us.

A girl who was in a coma.

A girl named Abby Donner.

She was the most recent piece of the puzzle.

Dad told me to wait for him in Bayou Malpierre, but he also said I had to talk to Abby Donner if she ever came out of her coma. Why? I don't know.

I don't know much, really.

Ronny tensed at the window.

I went to him. "What is it?" I whispered.

Peering between a pair of filthy curtains, I spied a shadow moving in and out of the light. It was a figure, tall and thick. "Oh, no, no, no . . ."

"Quiet," Ronny said.

"Can you see his face? Is it —"

"Quiet!" he snapped.

The figure moved out of view. I cocked my bad ear. Why were the voices so quiet? I turned my head. Where were they?

For minutes, we didn't move.

Then there was a click at the back door.

I heard the door swing open and tap against the inside wall of the kitchen. I couldn't breathe. My lungs burned. My heart hammered. I looked for a weapon, picked up the other half of Ronny's broom, and held it out like a bayonet.

Footsteps sounded heavily on the floorboards. Ronny crept behind the door, his pointed broom handle aimed high.

Thunk . . . thunk . . .

The door flew open.

THREE

Casualties of War

"Derek Stone . . ." A low voice rang through the darkness.

A shape teetered in the doorway, then fell forward, a dead weight at my feet.

"It's Bob Lemon!" I cried, rushing to him.

"Shhh!" said Ronny, at my side. He bent down and tilted the old man's head forward. A great breath came from his mouth.

"They're near —" Lemon whispered.

"What happened to you?" I asked. Only hours ago, Lemon had helped my father battle Cane on a streetcar so I could escape. "What did they do to you?"

"Hamburgers did this to me!" he gasped, clutching the front of his shirt. His heart. "But never mind that. The girl . . . the girl is awake. . . ." He began to cough.

"What do you mean?"

"The girl!" Lemon grunted. "Something happened at University Hospital. I heard it on the news."

It hit me. "You mean Abby Donner? The girl in the coma?"

"Your father told me about her. It was just on the radio. Something happened. She bolted out of her coma like magic. She's awake —" He grabbed his neck.

"You need a hospital," I said, pulling out my cell phone.

"Put that away!" Lemon said, slapping the phone closed. "Find that girl fast. If your father told you to, there's a reason."

He went silent. Ronny propped up Lemon's head with some old kitchen towels he'd found. The murmuring in my bad ear was growing louder, closer. When I pressed my ear to try to stifle the pain, I made out five voices moving toward us. Closing in.

"We only have a few minutes," said Ronny, sneaking toward the windows in the back of the house. "No more than that. Bob, we need to move you."

"He's right," I added. "You can't stay here. I'll call —"

"No!" Lemon said forcefully. "Wait until you're out of here. And don't use your cell. You can't have the police tracing the call and connecting this with the house fire. They'll pick you up. You have to stay free. Use a pay phone. There's a hotel three blocks down with one. You need as much of a head start as you can get."

He was right, we had to keep moving. But it still hurt to see him in pain. I had only known Big Bob Lemon for a couple of days. Hours, even. Yet here he was, risking his life for me, for the second time in one night.

"Your daddy tells you to do something, you do it," he added.

"Yes, sir," I said quietly.

I could tell from his eyes that he was doing everything he could not to pass out.

Ronny squeezed Lemon's shoulder. "Derek, we have to go. Now."

"That's right, go!" said Lemon. "Stay alive, Derek. You have to stay alive —"

Stay alive. It sounded like an order. A command.

Ronny yanked me onto the back steps. He scanned the dark. "Now!" he whispered. We ran from yard to yard out of the light, all the way to the corner. I didn't look back.

It was nearly three in the morning and the streets were empty when we reached the hotel. "I'll stay out here to watch and listen," said Ronny. "Hurry it up."

I pushed through the revolving doors and saw a bank of phones near the elevators. I went to them, digging in my pockets for change. I had none, but there was a sticker on the phone saying that emergency calls were free.

I dialed 911, and a woman answered. She said something, but I spoke over her. "Border Street. Number 13. A man is having a heart attack."

"Your name, please?" she asked.

"Number 13, Border Street," I repeated as clearly as I could. "And use your siren." I hung up.

Then I was back on the street with Ronny, where the dark swallowed us up again. We ran away from the voices. Why I heard them, or why I'd been hearing them for days, I can't tell you, but I heard them. They hissed, squealed, shrieked, converging on the house loud and wild.

"Ronny —" I started.

"I know," he said, tugging me firmly forward. "If we could go back to him, I would. We can't. We have to keep moving. Get to the hospital, find the girl, get to the bayou. So run. Now!"

Told you life was speeding up.

FOUR

Room 754

It didn't take us long to get to University Hospital, but we had to keep out of sight until morning. Places like that pay special attention to anyone who tries to enter in the middle of the night without an emergency. Can't say I blame them.

Finally, eight AM came around, gray and hot and wet. By the time Ronny and I stepped up to the emergency room doors, I was a ball of sweat. I pulled my shirt away from my skin and wafted air into it.

Ronny gave me a look. "Pretty gross," he said.

Times like these convinced me that Ronny wasn't completely gone. There were still traces of my brother in this person. Could he possibly come back?

"Wanna sniff?" I asked, grinning.

But Ronny wasn't with me anymore. His face had turned to stone. It was already over.

"Follow me," he said, pushing his way through the double doors like a robot.

I followed him into the ER. It was buzzing.

Along with everything else — the blaring intercoms and droning chatter from the waiting room and behind the admissions desk — there was some big deal going on. From what I could tell, it involved an older woman and a couple of nasty-looking guys, all on stretchers and all yelling at one another. I silently thanked them. Their disturbance was a good cover.

Ronny and I slipped through the ER lobby and into the main building. As we searched for the front desk, I wondered what I was actually doing there. What did I expect? Could I even begin to explain to this girl what I thought — what I knew — was happening?

Was I going to tell her about her mother? "Excuse me, miss, your mom died, but not really. She's kind of a zombie, totally dead, way crazy, and a killer."

Right. That would go over well.

"Big place," Ronny said, looking around. "We need the girl's room number."

"We could ask," I said.

Ronny eyed the front desk. A group of men and women with cameras and microphones stood in a bunch with two security officers. "Reporters," he said. "If we didn't get turned away, we'd be put with them."

That impressed me. He had sized up the scene quickly. "Maybe we could sneak a look at the computer behind the main desk. I think the patients' room numbers are on the computer screen."

Ronny scanned the desk, thinking. "Okay, but we need a distraction."

"Maybe do something dumb?" I suggested. "If you can distract someone, I can try to get the room number."

"Dumb? Like what?" he asked.

"Like, I don't know, dumb," I whispered.

Ronny's face changed slightly as if he had formed a plan.

He swiveled on his heels, then pulled me around a corner. I had no clue what he was doing until he found a supply closet, slipped in, and came out a minute later wearing a blue work shirt. He tucked some white garbage bags in his belt. He handed me a similar shirt.

"What are we, janitors?" I asked, pulling the shirt on. "Couldn't you find some extra scrubs? I always wanted to be a surgeon —"

My heart quickened. A surgeon?

I took up the silver blade. . . .

Stupid words from nowhere again.

When I snapped out of it, Ronny was already heading toward the front counter in the main lobby. He nodded to me and stepped right up to the desk. Grinning, he made a big thing of unflapping a garbage bag.

"For the trash run this afternoon, miss," he said to the woman standing behind the desk, charming her like a true country boy. The woman smiled and pulled her chair back.

"Here you go," she said.

But as Ronny reached for her wastebasket, he fumbled and dropped it. "Oh, miss, I'm sorry!"

It actually looked natural. The contents of the basket — papers and tissues — spilled on the floor under her desk.

"Oh, dear," the woman said, stooping to help him clean it up. While she was facing away, I leaned over and scanned the patient list on her computer. "Donner, Abby" was near the bottom of the alphabetical list on that screen. Our little reconnaissance mission was a success.

I stepped away from the desk as Ronny gathered the last of the trash. He grinned at the woman. "I'm real sorry, miss," he said.

"It's ma'am," she replied, smiling. "And it's no problem."

"You have a good day," Ronny said, handing me the garbage bag as we walked away.

"Room seven-five-four," I said. "That was pretty good, by the way."

He shrugged. "I guess I can be sneaky."

We wormed back through the halls together and found an elevator. I tossed the garbage bag in a nearby can before we got in.

When the elevator doors opened on the seventh floor, room 754 was to our left. I could hear the bubbling noise of televisions up and down the hall. I began to imagine the room, and the bed, and then her.

A new thought hit me.

What injuries had Abby Donner suffered in the accident? I had seen her being thrown all around the crashing train car with my own eyes. She could be completely busted up. Did she still have all her limbs? Was she scarred? Blind? Crazy over her mother's death? What?

Just then, Ronny stopped. His shoulders tensed. He tilted his head.

"What's the matter?" I asked.

"I'll be back in a minute. Find her." He moved down the corridor, turned the corner, and darted out of sight. The sounds of the hospital buzzed in my ears, but I didn't hear any voices. Did he?

I took a deep breath and suddenly felt completely empty. I imagined the face of the Coma Girl. I didn't want to do this. I didn't want to see her.

But my father had told me to, and my feet took me forward. I found room 754.

Remembering the horror of the train wreck, I raised my hand and knocked on the half-closed door.

FIVE

The Donner Girl

"Who is it? Grammy? Come in. I'm ready to go."

Her voice was bright. Not a dead voice. Not damaged.

My nerves were electric. I pushed on the door and stepped in.

She looked like I remembered her. Her face hadn't been damaged in the crash, though it was pale. Being in a coma for weeks would probably do that to a person. She was dressed in normal clothes — shorts, T-shirt — and sat cross-legged on the bed with a book in her lap. She looked surprised for a minute when I came in. Then she nodded to the corner.

"Sorry, I thought it might be my grandmother," she said. "The wastebasket's over there. It doesn't have much in it because I've been eating through a tube, but last night's pudding cup is in there, from my first meal after I woke up. I was really hungry, but my stomach couldn't handle it. Don't worry, I made it to the bathroom to throw up, but I tossed the rest of it out —"

"Abby Donner?" I said, pulling off the janitor's shirt like a superhero, though I felt exactly the opposite. "Do you remember me?"

She frowned. "Remember you? Well, I don't know about me and memory. . . ."

While Abby searched my face, I noticed that her arms were scratched up, and — I hadn't seen it before — her foot was in a cast.

All at once, her eyebrows shot up. "The boy from the train! You made it! You survived —" She closed her eyes quickly. When she opened them again, they were wet.

I felt my cheeks get red. "I'm sorry about your mother," I said.

"I . . ." She nodded a few times, stopped, swallowed, and wiped her eyes. "They already had a service. There wasn't any . . . they haven't found her yet."

Which I knew, of course. Her mother's body was still walking around out there.

Abby said nothing else right away. Looking into her eyes made me uncomfortable, so I glanced out the window. The city outside was quivering with heat; the river was brown and slow.

"Anyway," she said, trying to lighten things up, "I

popped out of my coma yesterday. A miracle, they say. They've been monitoring me for weeks, and I'm pretty much healed after the accident, so they're letting me out today. I have to check in every three days, but otherwise, I'm good. My grandmother's coming to bring me home."

I smiled. "That's good. Really good. My name is Derek, by the way, in case you don't remember."

"Right," Abby said. "Thanks for coming." Her forehead wrinkled. "But why did you come? I mean, I know we were in the same crash together, but it's not like we really know each other. We don't, do we? I'm a little fuzzy from my coma. . . ."

I breathed out. There was no choice — I started.

"Okay. So, listen. You're totally not going to believe any of this, but I have to tell you some really strange stuff that's been happening since the train wreck. Impossible stuff. I don't even believe it myself, except that I don't really have a choice —"

"Nice buildup," Abby said, laughing nervously. "Do you even *want* me to believe you?"

"Well . . . yeah . . ."

Her smile flickered and died. *Like a failing candle flame,* I thought. Stupid words.

"Okay then," she said softly. "Tell me."

Before I could say another word, Ronny dashed into the room, still in his janitor's shirt.

"Hey, a reunion of survivors! What, no shirt for me?" Abby said, grinning.

"Sure, sure." Ronny tried to smile at her, then pulled me aside. "Look, I don't hear any voices yet, but I still don't like it. You'd better make it quick. We can't be anywhere too long. I'll scout for exits." He was gone as quickly as he had come in, a soldier on a mission.

"Aside from his pasty complexion and bad hair," Abby said after he'd gone, "what's his problem exactly?"

Some lead-in. I took it.

"That's sort of what I wanted to talk to you about," I said slowly. "Since the crash, I've seen some of the people who died in it."

"You went to their funerals?"

"Uh, no," I said. "I mean, the people are still around."

"You mean, the survivors —"

"No," I said. "They died, all right. Only . . . they're back."

Abby narrowed her eyes at me. "They're back?"

"Yes."

"They died, but they're back."

"Right," I said.

She nodded. "And I thought *I* was crazy from my coma."

"Look, no," I said. "At least you're not dead. And neither am I. But . . . my brother Ronny is. Ronny died in the crash."

"But I just saw him."

I took a breath. "Now you get it."

Abby's face fell. Her silence gave me a chance to try to put everything into some kind of order.

I told her how Ronny died and showed up one day, changed; how I learned that an earlier train had crashed in 1938; how I came to know that the souls from the earlier crash had entered the bodies of several people in our crash; and finally how I discovered that Ronny was now inhabited by the soul of someone named Virgil Black.

I also told Abby the bad news — wasn't it all bad news? — that most of the souls were dangerous convicts, and that they were after me for some reason I couldn't explain.

Her mouth hung open through most of this. She finally closed it and spoke quietly. "Dead people are after you?"

"I don't know why," I said, looking down at the floor. "My father told me I know something, but it's hidden in my memory or something. Anyway, he also told me I had to find you if you woke up."

"Me? Why me?"

I shrugged. "I was kind of hoping you'd tell me.

Maybe it has something to do with you being in a coma?"

"Uh-huh. Maybe," she said. "But I'm not going back into it just for you."

I smiled a little, then took a deep breath. "You don't hear voices, do you?"

She spun around, slid off the bed, hobbled to the window, and looked out — all without saying anything. Then she turned to me again. Her face was red. "Voices? Of course not! You're nuts, is what you are. Dead people coming back? It doesn't happen that way. They're dead. *She's* dead. Everyone knows that. My mother died in the wreck and that's all there is to it. She died and she's dead and she can't talk to me!"

I stared at Abby, not quite knowing how to react to this outburst. All at once, the anger fell from her face. She covered it with her hands and started to sob.

"It can't be true!" she said. "It's not possible. She isn't . . ."

A shiver of fear entered my chest. "Abby, did you hear someone?"

"No, no, no . . ." She sniffled loudly. "She's dead!"

"Your mother?" I said quietly. "Have you heard her?"

Her eyes flashed at me. Then, slowly, she nodded.

Climbing back on the bed, she said, "Just so you know, I don't go for make-believe, I don't. My whole life, I never had imaginary friends. I never even hung out with kids who had imaginary friends. I never played with dolls. I like sure things, like numbers, history. You can depend on all that —"

Huh. That sounded familiar.

"Abby," I said. "Did you hear your mother's voice?"

She raised her red eyes. "I think she came to see me."

I tried not to react. "She —"

"She came to see me when I was in my coma. She talked to me. Told me things. I *heard* her when I was — wherever you are when you're in a coma. Grammy said the nurses even told her they saw someone here, a woman, but she disappeared before they could talk to her. I think it was my mother."

"What did she say?" I asked.

Abby shook her head sharply. "But I can't have heard her, right? Because she died in the crash. She couldn't have —" She stopped, her face stricken with sudden horror. "My mother's not . . . she isn't one of the . . . you haven't seen her?"

"No!" I lied. "No. No. Nothing like that." I didn't know what else to say. I wasn't ready to talk about that. She wasn't ready to hear it.

Abby slumped onto her bed again, eyes filling with tears. "I guess I must have imagined it, right?"

"Tell me what she told you," I said. "In your coma."

Crossing her legs as before, with her ankle cast in her hands, Abby grew very quiet, very still. "She told me about a place. It was dark all around. No. Not all around. There was a big flash of light above her. And she said everything was wet. Like they were standing in a dirty lake or something."

Ronny had told me the same thing: It was wet.

"Where was all this supposed to be?" I asked.

She shook her head. "I don't know. There were people around her. Lots of them."

Lots. The word sounded sickening. "Do you mean 'lots' like, 'Wow, this cereal has *lots* of raisins,' or like, 'Wow, there are *lots* of people in the world'?"

Abby thought about it, then took a breath. "Like there are lots of people in the world, only . . ." She paused. "Only more. They all wanted to go through the flash of light. But only a few made it."

The Rift, I thought. My heart dropped to my feet. I felt dizzy, trying to understand. "Were you and your mother . . . close?" I asked.

Abby frowned. "Of course we were close. She was all I had. Aren't you and your brother close?"

I said nothing.

"So what do you think it means?" she asked.

I paced to the window and back. "I don't know how you heard what you heard. But I think — I think it means that the dead are gathering and waiting for a chance to return."

"Return?" Abby's face turned even more pale. "The dead are waiting to return? What for?"

All I could think of was the War. I was trying to work up to telling her about it, but Ronny burst into the room.

"He's here," Ronny hissed urgently. "Cane. We need to go!" He turned and disappeared through the door again.

I heard a growl echoing in my ear. I turned to Abby. "We're leaving. And you're coming with us."

"Me?" she snorted. "I'm waiting for my grandma —"

More voices. "Sorry," I told her. "We can't wait for your grandmother."

Abby burst out laughing. "Are you serious? *Everybody* waits for my grandmother! I was at a wedding once, and the priest was at the altar, ready to do the vows. Everybody, and I mean *every*body, in the church was waiting and waiting —"

"Tell me while we run!" I snapped.

I grabbed her arm and charged out the door after Ronny.

SIX

Express Checkout

The hall was jammed with gurneys, doctors, patients. Ronny tore through them and bolted around the corner. I hustled Abby along after him as quickly as I could.

"No running!" yelled a nurse.

Among the tangle of voices in my ear, I heard Cane's terrifying murmurs. The others, too — hissing, grunting somewhere in the halls. They were here and closing in.

"How did they find us?" I called to Ronny.

He was already far down the corridor, flashing through a set of doors that swung closed behind him. He kept running.

"Come on!" I said, turning back to Abby.

"I have a broken foot, you know —"

For once, someone else was slower than me. We clomped down the hall. Abby slapped her hand on the electric opener, the doors whooshed back, and we barreled through.

I raced around the first corner to my left, slammed into a nurse, and knocked a lunch cooler out of her hand. She screamed.

"Sorry!" I said, as the cooler tipped over and opened. I bent over to pick up what I thought was going to be her sandwich.

It wasn't a sandwich. It was a lung.

My stomach heaved into my throat.

Abby grabbed my arm and yanked me into a stairwell. "That was classic!" she said, laughing.

"I just knocked over someone's transplant!" I cried.

"They'll probably just wash it off —" she started, when I clapped my hand over her mouth.

The short soldier — the one I called Twitchy — stormed down the hallway past the stair door, his head twitching like a squirrel's. The conductor was with him. His empty, ragged sleeve dangled at his side.

"Holy crow!" Abby whispered, pulling my fingers away. "Is that them? They look so —"

"Dead?" I whispered. "That's them."

People yelled down the hallway, telling the two dead men to stop. But they just walked on.

I thought we might be in the clear, until Cane moved past the doorway. His crazy smile looked like a crescent moon, half-cocked up the side of his face. I hoped Abby's mother wouldn't show herself. Not yet. Please. Not now —

A high-pitched squeal rang through the hallway. It pierced my bad ear. A hand thumped my shoulder, and I nearly jumped out of my skin.

It was Ronny. He pulled me and Abby down the stairs behind him. "Come on!"

"Ow, ow, ow," she said. "My foot—"

At the next landing, Ronny ran through the door and quickly found a service elevator on the sixth floor. We all piled in. The doors closed behind us.

Before the elevator moved, there was a sudden kick on the doors. Ronny backed up, his finger to his lips. We heard a garbled noise out in the hall, but the doors didn't reopen.

A low voice outside the elevator.

Not Abby's mother.

Ronny tilted his head as the elevator moved away from the sixth floor. "That's a new one. Someone else from the crash," he whispered.

"How do you know?" Abby asked.

Ronny didn't answer before the elevator lurched and slowed. The doors opened on the second floor, and we barreled past a couple of doctors in green scrubs before they had time to stop us. Ronny stormed down the hall as if he knew exactly where he was going. It was strange to watch him. Was it coming back to him now, everything he had learned as a fighter in the war down there?

We approached an open staircase, which led down to the main lobby.

"Grammy might be out front by now," said Abby, hobbling along like a champ.

"Except we can't go that way," said Ronny, suddenly yanking my arm nearly out of its socket. "Out the back."

We turned and raced down the hall to the rear of the building. We leaped down the stairs there as quickly as we could with Abby's ankle in a cast. At the bottom stood a door with a red bar across it.

Ronny didn't hesitate. He grabbed the bar with both hands and pushed. The alarm screamed in our ears as we dashed out to the parking lot.

Abby looked around frantically. "There!" she cried, pointing. "My grandmother!" She pushed me at a minivan driving slowly along the side of the hospital, toward the pick-up circle up front. "Grammy!"

The woman at the wheel slowed, spotted Abby, and waved.

"I made hospital friends!" Abby said, staggering over to the car with me and Ronny. She tugged open the side door and pushed us into the backseat, then hopped into the front, pulling her foot in behind her. "Guys, meet Grammy Nora. Now, hit it, Grammy!" yelled Abby. "To the floor!"

"But, dear —" the woman started. All it took was a glimpse of the four mangy figures charging out the door after us, and she slammed her foot on the gas. The car burned rubber all the way into traffic.

SEVEN

On the Streets of Metairie

If Abby's grandmother had a heavy foot on the gas, it wasn't any lighter on the brake.

No matter how quickly we screeched down the street, Grammy Nora made a complete stop at every red light and stop sign. It was like the pulse setting on a blender. We were hurled back and forth in our seats until we felt sick.

"Good thing I didn't eat that pudding," said Abby, under her breath.

"You boys," said Grammy Nora, scowling into her rearview mirror. "I don't think I like whatever it is that you're mixed up in."

Abby turned to look at me and Ronny. "I think it's just a little misunderstanding. Right, guys?"

"Absolutely," I said.

Grammy Nora didn't seem sold.

After zigzagging from one street to another, Ronny asked Grammy Nora to head for the alley behind Royal Street. We needed his car. The minivan turned onto an avenue that ran straight toward the French Quarter.

Finally, the voices faded from my ear.

The silence gave me a minute to think. I realized that the dead had managed to find us everywhere we'd gone since yesterday — the Quarter, the cemetery, the abandoned house last night, the hospital this morning.

I didn't like it.

If the dead really were following me, they were finding me.

I knew I needed lots of time to think this through, but I wasn't going to get it. We had just turned off the avenue and roared into a mess of short streets when Abby jumped.

"Stop!" she screamed. "Grammy, stop!"

"What?" Grammy Nora said, alarmed. "But Abby, this isn't anywhere —"

Abby pointed to a large house that sat on a hill behind a big black fence. "There!"

Abby pulled on the door handle before her grandmother even slammed on the brake. She swung herself out of the car, nearly tripped over the curb, hopped up to the iron fence, and strained against it.

I followed her.

Over a rise of lawn behind the fence stood one of the grander houses in the Quarter, a three-story brick mansion. It had a broad, peaked front and tall white columns, which ran up from a porch that stretched across the front and sides of the house. The bricks were painted dark pink, but they looked gray in the hazy light.

I glanced back at Grammy Nora. She shrugged. Ronny looked anxiously at me from the backseat of the van.

"Abby, do you know this place?" I asked.

For a long time she studied the house and said nothing. Then she shook her head slowly and backed away from the fence. "No. Not this house. But there's something about it. The columns?"

A brown shade rippled in an upstairs window. Someone looked down at us. Abby turned away.

"I don't know," she said, narrowing her eyes in concentration. "Something about a house, not this one, but *like* this one. Derek . . ." Abby turned to me. "Did she really come to me in the hospital? My mother?"

I almost shrugged, but then stopped myself. "I don't —"

"She's one of those people, isn't she? One of the dead ones. You can tell me. Please tell me."

I saw her mother's image in my mind. Gray-faced, soaked, her hair matted, her eyes as black as onyx marbles. She had a horrible, stuttering, maniacal walk, and a gargling voice. I only understood one thing she'd said to me.

Firsssssst . . . firsssst . . .

"Never mind," Abby said quietly, shaking her head. "I believe it anyway. The dead are gathering. I think I get that. And there's something about a house. And about you. They're after you."

"I don't know why," I said for the second time in an hour. It was almost a whisper.

"But your dad thinks I can help you," she added. "Because of what I know. But how?"

"Maybe it's because of your mother," I said. "Maybe *she* knows something, and maybe she told you."

"How does your dad know about my mom?" Abby asked.

It was a question I hadn't asked myself before.

Abby took my arm suddenly, and I jumped.

"I remember something else she told me!" she said. "It was garbled. I couldn't make out most of it. But there was one word I understood. I remember it now."

She stopped.

I glanced back at the van. Ronny's eyes were riveted on Abby. He opened the car door and walked over to us.

"What word?" he asked. "What word was it?"

She was shaking. "Legion."

My veins turned to ice.

"I know the word," said Ronny, staring off into the east, where the sun refused to rise. "I remember the Legion. It's what they call themselves. Their army."

The word spoke of the monumental dead, of souls that were centuries old, of soldiers marching forward in a war more horrifying than I could ever imagine.

Legion. The Grand Army of the Dead.

Abby's grandmother walked over to her and took her hand. "Dear, this is silliness. It's just your coma talking. Your mind was in and out. We nearly lost you —"

"That's when my mother came to me!" Abby said fiercely. "She came to the hospital!"

"Oh, Abby," said Grammy Nora. Her eyes pooled with tears.

"The Legion is coming here, soldier by soldier," said Ronny, still staring off into the distance. "It's evil against good. Evil is winning."

"But Abby," Grammy Nora said. "Dear, this is —"

Abby took her grandmother by the shoulders. "Grammy, no! He's right. They're both right. I heard it in my coma, only I didn't want to believe it. People are coming. Dead people."

The old woman paled, shocked by Abby's insistence, her flashing eyes and darkening features.

Finally, she nodded. "Yes . . . okay . . ." she stammered. "I believe you, Abby. But what are we supposed to do? What can we hope to —"

"Don't hope," Ronny snarled, more darkly than I'd ever heard him before. "There's no time for hope. Just run. Hide." He turned to me. "Derek, we have to go to Bayou Malpierre. Now. Maybe your father — our father — can tell us what to do next."

"Come, dear," said Grammy Nora, pulling Abby toward the car.

Abby looked at me. Ronny was already walking away.

"Good-bye," she said. "I don't know . . ."

I could tell her mind was racing. She was struggling to uncover things she hadn't remembered yet. They would haunt her until she did.

Like me and Ronny, she knew something we needed.

"Here's my cell number," I said, writing it down for her on a scrap of paper. "Call me if you remember anything else."

Grammy Nora put her arm around Abby and helped her back into the car.

As I watched them drive away, I hoped I'd see Abby again. But Ronny had just warned us against hope. So never mind. We had to go.

"Let's find my car," Ronny called over his shoulder. "Come on."

EIGHT

The Roof Angel

The day was still hazy but already burning hot as we headed into the Quarter. We knew Ronny's car was parked in the alley behind our house. We didn't know if it would still be drivable. We hadn't seen it since the fire.

"I hate this place," Ronny grumbled when we turned onto Royal Street. "I'll sneak around back and bring out the car. Stay hidden."

"Be careful —" I said, but he was already out of earshot. I let him go. He was hardly Ronny much anymore. The War had changed Virgil Black. Coming back had changed him, was changing him, every day he stayed here.

I was changing, too.

It was too much to think about. I was back in the Quarter for the first time in a day, staring at the ruins of the house that I'd lived in my whole life. The bottom story was charred, the front door and windows busted through and boarded up. The firefighters probably did that. The old red brick was stained with soot. It shot upward from the windows, like the ragged wings of a giant raven.

My eyes followed the burn marks up to the top floor and then to the *faux chambre* at the very top of the house. Dad's special room. Why my eyes were drawn to the angel ornament on the peak, I couldn't tell you, but my heart quickened with the sudden words that popped into my head.

I was . . . an angel child . . . child of light . . .

The ornament had survived the fire, but its wings and face were black with soot.

I watched a lone fireman walk gingerly across the roof. He carried an ax in his hand and peered in the broken windows of the secret room. He pulled away, then stomped his feet on the rooftop, answered the walkie-talkie on his belt, and stomped some more.

On top of my burned house.

The word *Legion* echoed in my head, like a pebble dropped in a steel drum. The Legion had destroyed my family, taken my house, forced me to run.

Don't hope? Just run and hide?

Would the Legion ever stop chasing us? Why should they? They needed people to die, so they would have more bodies to translate into. They fought me and Ronny because we knew about them. So I was on the run. It was more than that, but how much more, I didn't know.

Twice I turned away from my blackened house. Twice I turned back. Twice I stared at that charred angel and knew I had to have it.

I had to have it.

The fireman was out of sight now. In seconds, I was across the street. I knew the building on the corner had a fire escape on the side street, so I used it. I pulled my heavy body up to the roof and crossed over to the far side. It was a short, clumsy jump to the next roof, and the next, and then to mine.

I glanced around. Still no fireman.

I moved over to the *faux chambre* and peered in the windows. Burned books and old model trains were scattered everywhere across the wet, blackened floor. I wanted to cry. But there was no time. I eased myself onto the hidden room's roof from behind, afraid it wouldn't hold me, but not about to stop now. With one quick swipe, I grabbed on to the burned figure. It was five and a half inches of carved, gilded wood, now blackened by ash.

What I was going to do with the thing, I couldn't tell you. But the moment I held it, I felt totally, completely sure that this was right. Having the angel with me was right.

I unscrewed it from its base and stuffed it in the

side pocket of my cargo pants. I slid back down to the main roof and stood there, breathing heavily. You'd think I'd just run a race or something.

"So there, Legion," I said.

It probably wasn't my most mature moment. So what?

That word — Legion — coiled in my left ear like metal twisting, screeching, squealing. It was the same sound I'd heard in the hospital. I shook my head to clear it, but the sound didn't fade.

I pressed my finger on my ear to block the sound, but only changed it to a kind of high-pitched hissing.

"What *is* that?" I said aloud.

Suddenly, a window shattered in the little room, spraying me with shards of glass.

I screamed. She was standing in the room. Cane's wife. Abby's mother. Her hand had thrust through the glass at me. The smell of something rotting hit me like a wave. It was awful, like old meat or garbage.

"Get away!" I yelled, tripping over my own feet and landing on my back. Her face was gray and horrible, her eyes filthy, staring through me.

"First . . ." she hissed. *"Firssssst . . ."* It was the same word she had said at the diner near Bordelon Gap.

Her eyes bored into mine. Her head twitched back and forth, stringy hair dripping over her sunken cheeks. My ear felt like it was being skewered. I finally crawled to my feet, tripped, doubled over, and turned to the roof's edge.

Firsssst . . .

I got over to the next roof, and the next, and the next, and onto the fire escape, tripping and stumbling but not stopping until I was on the ground again. The shrieking stayed in my head.

"Stop!" I groaned, slapping my hands over my ears.

"Quiet down!" Ronny said, running up the sidewalk toward me. "Are you crazy? What are you doing?"

"Her!" I spat. I told him everything, wobbling on my feet.

He made a noise in his throat. "Cane's wife? In our house?" Ronny's face twisted. He spun on his heels, clutching my arm to keep me from falling over. "This is worse than I thought."

NINE

Driving

I staggered down the street next to Ronny. "How could she get into our house in the first place?" I asked.

"She's dead," he said, tugging on my arm.

"What was she doing there?"

"I don't know. Hurry up. I got a car."

"Your car's okay?" I asked.

Ronny snorted angrily. "No. It's not even there. It must have been destroyed, because the pavement where I left it is burned black. I found another car."

He slipped into an alley, turned left, then quickly headed on for two blocks. I could barely keep up. Ronny stepped over to an older sedan, pulled a set of keys from his pocket, unlocked the door, slid into the driver's seat, and pushed the passenger door open.

"Get in," he said.

I did. Ronny started the car. We roared to the end of the block and sped out of the Quarter.

"Ronny, did we just steal this car?"

"Borrowed," he said.

"Borrowed?" I repeated. "From who?"

"From her," he said. "Sam . . . Samantha."

"What? Your old girlfriend?" I asked. The last time Ronny had seen her, she had left in tears.

"The car was parked on the street behind her house. I remembered that she always kept her keys in it." He breezed around a corner.

"You remember that?" I said. "That Samantha left the keys in her car? Really? That's Ronny stuff. There's still some of you left!"

"It's a mess in here," he said, tapping his forehead.

I knew that, of course. But I also liked knowing that Ronny — my brother — was still in there somewhere.

I suddenly caught a whiff of something bad, and I guessed that some critter had crawled under Sam's backseat and died there. How long had it been since she had even used the car? It struck me that Ronny needed to call Sam and tell her that we "borrowed" her car, so she wouldn't file a police report. We didn't have time for the police.

Ronny agreed, so I dialed the number and put my cell on speakerphone.

"Hello?" a voice answered. "Derek?"

"No. This is Vir — Ronny," Ronny said.

A pause. "Oh. Hi."

"Uh," he said, "I took your car."

"What?" Sam said.

"Borrowed. I borrowed your car. We need it. Me and Derek. For a little while. I'll bring it back later. I promise."

There was silence, then Sam said, "Take your time, Ronny. I know you're sorting some things out. I don't need the car right now. My dad can . . . Just take your time. The tires are a little low. Be safe."

Ronny stared at the phone. His eyes started to well up. I couldn't tell what was going through his mind, but the last thing I needed was for him to be crying at the wheel. I turned off the speaker and held the phone to my good ear.

"Thanks, Sam," I said. "Ronny says thanks."

"Okay," she replied sadly. "Take care of him, Derek, okay? Bye."

As I hung up, Ronny groaned under his breath and set his eyes firmly on the road. It hurt to hear how much Sam missed him. Even I could tell that. They had been close, but since he came back, Ronny had been so cold. He treated her as if he didn't know her. Which he kind of didn't.

Should I have told Sam what was actually going on? Translation? The Rift? The walking dead? Ronny and Virgil?

No. Sam was normal. A nice person. She wasn't in this, not like us. Not even like Abby.

At least having the car bought us some time. I just didn't know how much. Between the streetcar incident, the fire, and the hospital, the police had to know that something weird was happening. I mean, someone must have noticed how everyone who "died" in the train crash was suddenly around again. Or they would notice it soon.

If the police dragged me and Ronny back to New Orleans, the fight would be over. We'd never be able to explain things in a way that anyone would believe. Not to mention that they'd do tests on Ronny and realize he was, uh, not really alive.

Total freak show.

No. We had to keep moving.

The smell was getting worse in the heat, so I reached back and opened the rear windows of the car. The air was hot and wet, but at least it moved.

We were deep in morning traffic when my cell phone rang. The sound of Abby's voice on the other end sent a shiver through me. And not a bad shiver, either.

Ronny was watching me.

I pointed to the road ahead.

"I . . . remember something else," Abby said.

There were people talking in the background on her end. I wondered where she was.

"My mom told me something about the house," she said. "Not the one we saw, but that reminded me. She said something about a red house."

A red house. That didn't do anything for me. "Where is it?"

"I don't know," Abby said. "But I think the Legion is trying to find something. And maybe it's this house, wherever it is. I'll call you if I remember more."

There was yelling in the background now.

"What's going on?" I asked. "Where are you?"

"Home." She paused. "The police are here. They said that the morning after the train accident, the rescue crews spotted my mom —"

Oh, no. "What?"

"Her body, on the rocks," Abby said. "Far down the chasm."

On the rocks. That's where Ronny said he had died.

"But when the last search crew got down there, she wasn't there. They're saying the body must have fallen into the river and got washed away. Grammy is having a fit."

Should I tell her now? "Abby —"

"Nice, huh? I gotta go."

Before I could say anything, she hung up.

How long would it be before Abby learned the whole truth? There would be no way to sugarcoat it. Her mother died. Then she . . . *un*died.

About an hour southeast of New Orleans, as we were driving along the highway, Ronny turned to me.

"Listen," he said, "did you and Ronny . . . I mean . . . were you friends? Besides being brothers?"

Where did that come from?

"I had friends back in Shongaloo," he added.

Shongaloo. That word conjured up what I imagined Virgil Black's life had been like in 1938, before he died. He'd actually *had* a life. He'd had friends. I could only imagine what a mess all this was in his head. He was probably hoping to sort it out.

I tried to think of how to answer, but I couldn't. It was all too much. "Yeah, Ronny and I were friends. But that's over now," I said. "I just want to find Dad and try to make everything stop."

Ronny nodded, said, "That's fine," and went quiet.

My throat burned. I hated shooting him down, knowing that there might not be another moment like this one. But I also hated that Ronny was gone.

I didn't want to talk.

When a state police cruiser roared past us, I realized it was the third one I'd seen. We decided to get off the highway and take local roads from then on.

The day was sopping wet and burning hot, even through an overcast sky. It was just after noon when the land thinned out and the wetlands began.

Focusing as far off in the hazy distance as I could, I saw a dark mist rising off the waters that leaked into the Gulf of Mexico.

My chest ached. I was here again.

Bayou Malpierre.

TEN

Mist off the Water

Ronny slowed the car and suddenly pulled off the road. Other than some distant clumps of trees, there was nothing but flatland around us. Without the breeze, that awful odor filled the car again. The same smell from the roof of my house. The same smell as Cane's wife.

"What's the matter?" I asked.

Ronny held his index finger in front of his face, staring at it. It was the finger he had almost cut off while shaving. The tape I had used to bandage it was black with grime.

"What about it?" I said.

He raised the finger to his nose. "It took me a couple of hours to figure it out," he said. "This is what stinks." He peeled the soiled tape off, and I sucked in a gasp.

His fingertip was just as black as the bandage.

Taking the tip into his other hand, he twisted it

slowly until, with a sound like Velcro ripping, it broke off.

"Ronny! Oh, gawww —"

Turning the nib in front of his eyes, Ronny said, "How long am I going to be here? What's next, do you think? An ear? A foot?"

I didn't know how to answer.

He looked at me. "I sometimes wonder — did I ask to come back here? Did I volunteer to keep fighting? Because I don't even know. I don't want to be here."

I swallowed. It barely went down. "I'm glad you came back," I said quietly.

"I wish I'd never left Shongaloo."

"I know," I said. "But I'm glad you're here. With me."

He dropped his eyes and nodded. "That's it, then."

Ronny held the blackened tip of his finger for a minute, staring at it. Then he tossed it out the window, shoved the car in gear, and raced off.

My mind raced, too. What *would* happen to Ronny? Was he falling apart? What would be next? Why did his dead finger smell the same as Cane's mad wife? She died *on the rocks*. So did Ronny. Did that mean anything? Why didn't the others smell like that?

I had no answers.

We drove another half hour in silence. The heat was making me sleepy, until Ronny swerved the wheel. We rolled into a thickness of live oak and hunched cypress trees, all heavy with vines and wet moss.

Bayou Malpierre was a small area off the tail end of the Atchafalaya, a tributary of the Mississippi River. For centuries, the Atchafalaya's spillover had driven into the shallow land and flooded it. It had been overgrown and overcrowded by a forest of cypress and oak trees, moss and mangroves, vines and every kind of swampy vegetation you could imagine.

The deeper we went into it, the more forest grew around us. Soon it closed out the hazy sky altogether. Moving into the bayou was like falling into a place that hadn't changed for a hundred years. A thousand. A million.

Webs of green-black moss hung in tatters from cracked and bowed branches. All around us, sodden tree trunks grew out of — and died back into — pools of oil-dark water.

Something flashed across my mind. A memory. A place.

Five trees, broken and bent, stood in a half circle. Their thick limbs crisscrossed one another to form a kind of natural vault over a clearing that spread out on the soggy ground like an altar. Was that here? In Bayou Malpierre?

Would I see it again? What did it mean?

Ronny swerved the car quickly to avoid a tree stump, then plunged into a tunnel of low trees without slowing down.

"Careful!" I yelped. "It's not a tractor, you know!"

The squeal of branches scraping the car on both sides sent a chill up my spine. I hoped Sam would forgive us for making such a mess of her car.

Hope. That word again.

But that was the old Derek thinking. A banged-up car would mean less than nothing in a war against the dead. So skip it. Keep going.

Soon, we found ourselves on a narrow, rutted path. The tree branches hung low, scraping the car roof.

"We can't drive anymore," Ronny said, stepping on the brake.

When he cut the engine, we heard rumbling far off among the trees. It came from somewhere beyond what we could see.

"Come on," Ronny said. He climbed out of the car, slammed the door, and shoved the keys into his pocket.

We made sure the car was mostly hidden, then slowly pressed forward through the jungle. No more than half a mile later, I was surprised to see three open flatboats motoring slowly out behind a levee, a continuous mound of earth designed to protect lowlands from flooding.

"Look at them," I said, stopping to watch.

Ronny eyed the boats, saying nothing.

Each of the boats had fifteen or twenty passengers crowded against the railing. They were all in cargo shorts and wore sun hats and dark glasses. It seemed like they were having some kind of party. Some held cameras, others leaned over and dipped their hands into the water.

"Tourists," I said, "heading into the bayou for a happy ride among the wonders of nature."

"Uh-huh," Ronny grunted.

I hated the bayou. Dreaded it. But as laughter rolled across the water, I found myself feeling comforted by the sight of real people enjoying themselves. These tourists, acting so normal, made me feel oddly hopeful, as if we had left all the craziness back in New Orleans. As if those wild streets, the haunted cemetery, the dark alleys, the marching dead, would just stay back there.

As if the rising of the dead was a city thing.

Then Ronny scowled. "How nice for them to know nothing about a horror they could never imagine anyway."

My small sense of hope shriveled up and died.

The tour boats moved on, the sound of the motors faded, and I felt alone again.

"Let's keep moving," said Ronny.

Before long we saw a house, if you can call it that. The place was only a little larger than a doghouse, but less well built, on a narrow spit of land nearly surrounded by stagnant green water. It was basically a shack of four walls topped by a corrugated tin roof, higher on one side than the other like a shed. The whole thing was perched seven or eight feet above the sodden ground on posts that looked like hen's feet.

"Chicken shack," said Ronny.

"I'll say."

Ronny looked at me funny. "No, I mean it's actually a chicken shack. I used to build those in Shongaloo."

Virgil again.

I saw flies buzzing in and out of the single open window. Maybe there was discarded food inside. Maybe even a corpse. It made my throat thicken to think about it. A filthy shack, in the middle of nowhere with unspeakable insides.

But the more I stared at it, the more the feeling haunted me that this wasn't the first time I had seen the place. I felt the heavy spell of the swamp fall on me.

"I've been here before," I said.

"Lucky you," said Ronny dryly.

A boat horn echoed harshly across the open water.

I turned. "What is –"

Suddenly, an airboat – an aluminum flatboat with a giant propeller fan spinning in the rear – soared over the side of the levee, coiled through the air, and slammed to the ground, headed right for us.

ELEVEN

Finding What's Missing

The airboat shuddered to a stop a foot away from me. The propeller blades whirred to a standstill. Quiet fell over the bayou.

I really didn't need the added drama of almost being run over.

The airboat's driver said nothing. He was a man about my father's age, dressed in a T-shirt, grimy overalls, and a ragged baseball cap. He narrowed his eyes at me and Ronny, then spit off the side of the airboat.

I didn't like the look of him. Even after nearly driving over us, he seemed so calmly planted to his seat. He just stared at us and said nothing.

Ronny and I waited.

"Is one of you boys Derek Stone?" the man asked finally.

Oh, boy. "Uh . . . "

"Who wants to know?" interrupted Ronny.

"If one of you is," the man went on, showing two missing teeth up front, "I'm Smitty Fouks. Most people call me Bonton. Your daddy asked me to leave some flowers at an old tomb in the city. He said you'd understand. If one of you's him, I guess you did. Your daddy'll be here by nightfall."

I took a step forward. "I'm Derek. My dad's really coming?"

The man eyed me up and down. "I said he was, didn't I?"

I didn't like the way he spat again after he said that.

He continued. "But first, Waldo's missing. Weather's uncertain. We got to find him. Climb on in."

Ronny held me back. "Who's Waldo?" he asked.

Bonton looked Ronny up and down. I wondered if he noticed his missing fingertip. "Waldo's my precious boy."

The words sounded odd.

"And?" said Ronny.

"Waldo wandered off," the man went on. "The bayou's like his own big, wet yard. He could be anywhere. I got to find him before it gets dark. There might be rain."

Ronny's cold hand was still on my arm, holding me back.

"Can you help me look?" Bonton pleaded, patting the seat next to him as if he expected us to jump right in.

I hated the water. I wanted to stay on land and wait for my father. Plus, this guy was like some crazy caricature. I didn't know whether to trust him.

"Waldo's out there," he said, peering into the trees.

I glanced at Ronny. He shared my look. I guess we both silently agreed that if Dad wasn't coming until later, there was no reason not to help Bonton. Dad knew him, after all. What else were we going to do?

So Ronny and I climbed into the airboat and strapped in next to the man. He spit a third time and pushed a green button with his thumb. The propellers roared behind us.

"Hold on!" he hollered.

I was thrown back in my seat when we shot off the wet ground and hit the water. As the boat bounced along, I remembered just how much I hated the bayou.

We drove under a tangled cascade of vines and into a slightly broader, weaving waterway, picking up speed with every moment. Soon we came upon the tour boats Ronny and I had seen earlier. Now the passengers were singing to recorded music.

Bonton growled as we passed. "City folk, hoping

to catch a glimpse of the glory of the bayou. They don't know anything about it. Waldo laughs when the guides tell those people wrong things. He's a seer, Waldo is."

"A seer?" I said. "What do you mean?"

Bonton drove fast, and wind blew in our faces, stifling our words. He turned to look at me, then banked left out of the main waterway into a denser system of coiling tributaries. He cut the engine to a lower speed.

"My precious boy sees things before they happen," he said. "He knows things that the rest of us don't. Six years ago, during the big flood, that's when he got his insight. He loves this here bayou. Never been out of it. Of course, being a seer doesn't always help him know where he's going all the time. Some days, he just gets lost."

If I wasn't sure about Bonton, I really wasn't sure about his precious Waldo. Was Dad really friends with this guy? And why did we have to meet here? Dad knew how much I hated this place.

Bonton eased the airboat deeper into the swamp, among the massive trunks and tiny islands. He steered with one hand, shifting, pedaling the brake, and throttling through the tall reeds. I glanced at Ronny. I could tell he hadn't made up his mind about the man yet, either. I asked Bonton how he knew my father.

"Your daddy and me go way back," he said in a slow drawl. "I've lived in the bayou forever. He sold me three boats over the years. I only have this one left. He took a shine to my precious little boy, too."

That word was getting on my nerves. Ronny snorted and looked away.

"Your daddy'd stop here every few months to check on me and my boats, and he'd bring a little toy for Waldo. My boy sure loves those trains."

Trains?

In my mind I saw the scattered, broken, burned trains in my father's rooftop study. Then I pictured Abby's dead mother reaching for me, and the wooden angel in my pants pocket.

"What trains?" I asked, even though I knew.

"Your daddy brought him toy trains."

I felt ashamed that Dad had found someone who appreciated his love of trains more than Ronny and I did.

"Nice," I said. I didn't mean it.

Bonton went quiet as we reentered the waterway and circled into the swamp a second time. Nearly an hour had gone by and the sky was darkening with clouds. Fifty feet to our left, we could see more of the levee that Ronny and I had passed earlier. The earthen wall was ten or twelve feet high at this point.

It looked like an enormous grassy snake, slumbering in the water and nearly buried by dense tree cover.

"Every few years, when there were heavy rains, the bayou would flood," Bonton said, keeping his eyes fixed on the crest of the earth wall. "So we got a brand new dike, to ease excess water into the bayou nice and slow. You understand?"

"Like a lock," said Ronny. "It regulates the flow of water."

"That's right," said Bonton. "In a little moment, you'll see our very own lock gate!"

As we drifted along the levee, I followed it with my eyes to where the wall was interrupted by two thick cement posts, each about three feet wide. Between the posts was an iron slab divided in the middle. It looked like a set of dungeon doors. Something moved there, on top of the wall.

Bonton shouted, "There he is! Waldo!" He shut off the engine. "I should have known! That boy loves our new dike. He likes to dangle his toes in the deep side. Say, Waldo!"

I saw the boy clearly now, sitting on top of the iron slab. He was a little figure in green overalls and no shirt, facing away from us. He looked about six years old at most, with blond curls all the way to his shoulders. I could see why his father called him his "precious" boy. From behind, he looked like a cherub in overalls. And he seemed to be talking to someone I couldn't see.

"Waldo!" Bonton called. "Hey, Ralph Waldo Fouks!"

So that was his name? Weird.

The boy did not turn when his father called.

"How old is Waldo?" asked Ronny.

"Eleven," Bonton said.

Eleven! My eyes went wide. Waldo looked no more than five or six.

"Is he talking to someone on the other side?" I asked.

"No one to talk to out here," said Bonton. "He's just deep in himself. He's like that sometimes."

We drifted as close to the wall as we could. I watched Waldo's hand moving back and forth across the top of the metal slab. As we neared, I saw a toy train in his hand.

"Choo! Choo-choo!"

"Silly boy," said Bonton, grinning. "He doesn't even sense the danger of sitting on that dike. This bayou's fed by the Atchafalaya River and the Red River before that. The Red River can rile up fierce in a sudden rain."

Ronny leaned toward me. "You know where else the Red River runs?" he whispered.

My heart skipped a beat. Of course I did. "Bordelon Gap."

Bonton cupped his hands around his mouth and called up to the tiny boy. "Waldo! Waldo . . ."

The little figure stiffened, then turned slowly. Waldo was definitely small for his age, there was no doubt about that. But his face was — I don't even know how to say it.

Precious boy?

I couldn't imagine a brighter, happier face, especially out here in the sticks. Waldo's cheeks were pink, his eyes wide, and he had a great big smile on his lips.

"Poppa Bonton!" he said with a warm laugh. "But you aren't alone, are you, Poppa?" His voice was soft and melodic, as if he were reciting a poem. "Is that Derek Stone with you?"

Ice ran through my veins. I shook it off.

"I bet it is!" Waldo went on. "Derek! I'm happy to meet you!"

Ronny made a noise under his breath, but me — I don't know why — I couldn't help but smile at the precious boy.

"Happy to meet you, too," I said.

TWELVE

Little Boy Down

Bonton kept his eyes on his son while he spoke to us. "Would you boys mind . . ." He pointed to the levee and trailed off.

"You want us to help him down?" asked Ronny.

"It's my leg," Bonton explained, slapping his left thigh. I noticed that his leg was crooked and several inches shorter than the right one. It ended in a large black boot. "I broke it in three places during that old flood. It only healed in two. Plus, this here foot's not even real!"

He slapped the thick prosthetic boot. It made a hollow sound, and I couldn't help shivering. I needed to toughen up.

"I guess," I said, though I had no idea how to get up a twelve-foot-high embankment. I wondered how little Waldo had climbed up there in the first place.

Ronny and I jumped down to a narrow path running along the earthen wall. Ronny did all right getting up the levee, but it wasn't an easy climb for me. Twelve feet is higher than you think. Especially when you're hauling extra weight and are terrified of water. Bonton kept offering Waldo encouragement, telling him not to worry, help was on the way. I wanted him to throw a little of that encouragement my way, but I wasn't about to say that.

The boy had been quiet during our climb, but when we came close, he hooted, "Chugga-chugga-choo!"

Then he laughed. It sounded like the jangling of tiny bells. The closer I got, the more I could see that Waldo was a lot like a feather — frail and thin. He looked like a foundling or an orphan, the way his too-long overalls were cuffed up to his knees.

"They're coming, Waldo," called Bonton. "Soon now!"

Waldo smiled. "I'm being rescued!"

As I worked my way slowly across the top of the wall, I discovered that even though the water level on the bayou side was low, the water on the far side lapped all the way up to Waldo's dangling, shoeless feet.

Waldo turned his bright little face right to me, his hair a golden waterfall. I'll never forget it. Dabbed on his rosy cheeks were what looked like grains of powder, and his lips were red, but only in the center, as if he'd been eating berries.

But as odd as that was, my heart skipped when I looked into Waldo's eyes. From a distance, they had seemed radiant, sparkling. Up close, his eyes were blank, empty, and fixed on the distance over my shoulder. They didn't move at all.

Waldo was blind.

Ronny saw it, too, and gasped. "You can't . . . see . . ." he stammered.

"I know what you're thinking," Waldo said. "And it's true. I'm blind as a bat!" I looked down at the water, and my legs tingled. *Get it together, Derek.*

"So how did you get all the way up here?" I asked, focusing on the boy to distract myself.

Waldo smiled shyly. "I know my bayou, every inch of it. I feel like I've known it for a hundred years. More!"

I noticed then that his teeth were tiny little nibs. Baby teeth? Waldo was eleven years old with baby teeth? I shuddered a little.

"Home, Waldo?" Bonton hollered from below us.

"Yes, Poppa!" Waldo went on. "But let's not forget my rowboat. It's right . . . there!" He swiveled slowly and pointed away from us, as if he could see with his blank eyes. Right where he pointed was a beat-up little boat, tethered to a stump on the shallow side of the levee. Bonton chuckled, limped along the levee path, dragged the rowboat to his airboat, and tied it fast as we climbed back down to the airboat. Waldo was amazingly surefooted for a little kid who couldn't see. I tried not to let him show me up, even though I kept picturing myself tumbling down into the murky bayou of my nightmares.

Once we'd all made it back to the boat, Waldo said, "Now, home!"

Bonton motored up and turned the airboat around.

"Are we in the waterway now, Poppa?" Waldo asked, sniffing the air.

"You guessed it, son," said Bonton.

Waldo looked at me with his blank eyes. "Some places, the water gets deep," he said. "I hear tour guides say ten feet. That's not right. Thirty, fifty feet, even more in some places, even this side of the levee. Some places go all the way down —"

"All the way down?" asked Ronny. "To what?"

Waldo's little face beamed. "To . . . whatever!"

I felt like my atoms were spinning out of control, and I'd scatter into a trillion pieces. I tried to focus on seeing Dad soon, but couldn't. Why did he choose this faraway place to meet us, anyway? Everything about it creeped me out.

As we turned into the swamp near the shack, Waldo jumped in the seat next to me. "Look there, Derek!" he said. "Look!"

About a hundred feet away, nearly buried by a mess of vines and growth that kept me from seeing it before, were the remains of an ancient cemetery.

Its tombs were half submerged. Set in little streets like the cemeteries back home, the crypts were broken, crumbling into the black water. Their pitted white stone was blackened by mold.

"That boneyard's a hundred fifty, two hundred years old," said Bonton. "Used to be on dry land, but that's the way things go in Malpierre. Down and down and, finally, down. The bayou keeps getting deeper, breathing, like it's alive."

If they stood at all, the old tombs stood only because they leaned on their neighbors. Dark water lapped halfway up the crypts' doors, many of which had cracked open. Waves washed inside the resting places. My stomach turned.

I shivered. "The bodies . . ."

"Are where the bayou takes them!" said Waldo cheerfully.

I imagined the open stone cases. The waterlogged bodies. The water moving over them.

We motored slowly past the Venice of the dead, frozen as it collapsed. I wanted to turn away. Waldo kept his face on it for as long as he could, though, as if his blank eyes could see.

When we reached the shack, Bonton parked the airboat with the rowboat in tow, and we climbed down.

At once, Waldo froze in place, thrust his head toward the sky, and whooped loudly.

"Waldo, are you seeing something again?" asked Bonton.

"I'm feeling it, Poppa," said the boy, his face jerking one way then the other. "The rain!"

Even before he finished laughing, the sky cracked open. It began to pour.

THIRTEEN

In the Shack

A gash of lightning sliced across the haze. Rain came down like bullets. The air turned black.

We hurled ourselves up the shaky steps and into Bonton's shack seconds before a second bolt of lightning crashed overhead.

Being in the shack's single room was hardly better than being outside. The rain battered the roof like gunshots — *bang-bang-bang!* — causing leaks in a dozen places. Just like in the old house in New Orleans, the floor was soaked.

But the strangest part was watching Waldo.

He stayed out in the rain longer than the rest of us and came in sopping wet. Then he moved across the room with his hands out, not to feel his way around, but to find where water was dripping from the ceiling. Once he found a place that poured like a spout, he giggled, sat down under it, and turned his face up into the little stream. The water dripped from his forehead to his chin, streaking his cheeks. Again, his laugh was like bells.

I shared a look with Ronny. "That's normal," he whispered, making a face.

All the while, Bonton's eyes never left his son. He never stopped smiling. "What a child!"

"So, when do you think my dad will come?" I asked over the pounding rain, trying to get back on track. I didn't like the way Bonton shook his head.

"I had said soon, but after sunset's always a hard time to enter the bayou," he said with a snort. "Double, when it storms. Easy to get lost. We wrap ourselves in at night, don't we, Waldo?"

"Yes, sir!" said the boy brightly, fluttering his eyelids into the sputtering raindrops. "And it's looking like a you-know-what kind of night!"

"What kind of night is that?" Ronny asked warily.

I wasn't sure I wanted to know.

Bonton winked at his blind son, who, oddly, appeared to wink back. Maybe it was just a blink. "Waldo, how about you favor us with the story?"

Waldo nodded. "Surely, Poppa." He opened his mouth to the rain once more, then shifted over to Ronny and me.

"On a rainy night in the bayou, you might see her.

You might see *Bellamina.*" He paused, waiting for us to react.

We took the bait.

"Bellamina?" Ronny said.

"Who's she?" I asked.

"*She* is a *what*!" said Waldo gleefully. "*Bellamina*'s a big old steamboat!"

"From a time long forgotten, except in these parts," added his father. "A hundred and fifty years ago or more —"

"More!" Waldo said, as the rain pounded harder. "*Bellamina* was a side-wheeler, painted black from her hull all the way to her top deck. She could sneak around without anybody seeing her. But me? I saw her!"

Bonton's eyebrows shot up. "You saw her?"

"No, that was a lie," said Waldo quickly. "I never saw her. But *Bellamina* went all up and down the Atchafalaya. She was the floating home of a gang of smugglers! Oh, they were bad. They did away with folks who got in their way. Their captain —"

"Oh, now, I don't like this part," Bonton cut in, shaking his head quickly. He limped over to the door, looked out at the battering rain, then closed the door more tightly. "But you tell it, Waldo. You tell it."

"Their captain was a murderer," the boy went on,

his voice lowering, "and a poor cripple who never left his boat. The *Bellamina,* she was the terror of the Atchafalaya for years. But she was never caught, until one night a flash flood drove her into Malpierre. Drove her right here!"

Waldo moved his hands around him as if smoothing an invisible tablecloth. "And she sank, the *Bellamina* did. The crew would follow their captain anywhere. He couldn't leave his boat, so neither did they. They died on it. Folks say that every time it rains, the *Bellamina* could rise again. I bet we'll know it when she does."

"How?" Ronny asked. Thunder clapped outside, loud and booming.

Waldo kept smiling in my direction. "Because of the dogs! The captain kept a pack of dogs. They were wild, but they'd obey him. Dogs, Derek."

Dogs, Derek?

Did Waldo know about the dogs that chased me?

"They say that when the *Bellamina* sank, the dogs were hunting on shore, separated from their master," said Waldo, his voice lowering even more. "They starved and died here. They've haunted the bayou ever since. They'll howl when she rises again!"

The boy paused, almost as if he were waiting for someone to speak. No one did, until Bonton wobbled to the door a second time. He cracked it open and peered out while rain blew in on us. "That black boat can't rise anymore," he said. "Not since they built that lock. Malpierre's not deep enough now to float anything that big."

Waldo opened his mouth to drink the water dripping from the ceiling, and giggled like bells again. "It sure isn't," he said. Then he stiffened, letting the rainwater pour down his chin. "Oh, Poppa!" he called, turning to the door.

"Yes, Waldo, what is it?" Bonton asked.

"I see . . . water. Dark water. And —" Waldo grasped my arm tightly. "It's coming!"

I wanted to shake the boy's hand loose, but an alarm shrieked in the distance and echoed through the dense trees.

Bonton pushed past me and looked out into the rain. "No, no," he said.

"What is it?" I asked.

"That's the alarm bell at the lock," Bonton explained hurriedly. "One of the levees upriver has been breached. Maybe more than one. The river's gonna be wild. There could be a flood coming our way!"

I looked at Ronny. Ronny looked at Bonton. Bonton looked at Waldo who, swallowing more rainwater, began to laugh.

FOURTEEN

It Begins

Everything happened at once. Thunder crashed like bombs, followed by the faraway sound of splintering wood. The house shook on its peg legs. Bonton hobbled on his one real leg like a man possessed. "Thanks to you, Waldo, we'll have time to warn those tour boats!" he cried. "Malpierre surges in a flood. Those drivers need to know the safe way out. Derek, Ronny, come with me. Waldo, you stay here!"

"Yes, Poppa," the boy said calmly. "You know I will."

While the shack trembled like a shoebox on toothpicks, Bonton hopped down the stairs to the airboat.

Ronny followed him out into the rain. "Derek!" he called back to me.

I lurched to the door, but Waldo's fingers were still wrapped around my wrist. "Don't leave me, Derek, I'm scared!"

"Derek!" Ronny shouted. "Come on –"

"Hold on!" I yelled back.

The sky thundered again and again.

"We have to go!" called Bonton, his voice receding.

"Ronny! Ronny!" I yelled, making my way to the door and dragging Waldo with me. I struggled to keep the door open. Wind and rain whipped my face, while Waldo clung to my wrist. He wasn't letting go. His blank eyes searched my face. It was almost like he was trying to read my thoughts.

The airboat's engine roared over the sound of the storm.

"Ronny!" I called. "Don't leave me here!"

But the airboat disappeared into the bayou.

"The water's rising, isn't it?" Waldo asked calmly, as a wave crashed against the pilings under the shack. "Just like I said it would. It was already deep behind the lock."

There was a sudden crack, and the floorboards split enough that I could see the water flooding beneath us. I fell and slid across the floor. Waldo managed to stay on his feet, still holding on to me.

"We need to get out of here!" I said. "The house will crumble with us inside it —"

Thunder crashed again. The walls shook.

"Yes, Derek," Waldo said, not easing his grip or showing any sign of panic.

I crawled to the door. The front steps had twisted off the little shack and were floating away, a crumpled mess. I yanked my wrist from Waldo's hands and dropped straight down into the water, trying not to think about it. It came halfway to my knees. Waldo jumped down next to me, and the water reached his waist. The rain pounded us heavily. I could barely see.

I took a step, slipped, steadied myself, and reached for the boy, but Waldo made a sudden noise and quickly scuttled away.

"Waldo!" I cried out.

I struggled after him. The rain came down like bullets on my face, arms, back. Vines whipped around madly in the wind. "Waldo! Get back here!" I yelled. The water was rising faster now. I couldn't tell where to step. Then I heard a cry. Or maybe a laugh. I saw Waldo climbing into his rowboat.

"Where are you going?" I called into the storm.

He didn't hear me, or didn't want to. Was he going to paddle his dumb little boat in this rainstorm? Where did he think he was going?

"Waldo!" I cried.

No answer. Only that strange laugh of his. I urged myself through the storm after him. It felt like pushing a statue through mud. I waded from tree to tree, water beyond my knees now, trying to keep his rowboat in sight. Then a voice called out from somewhere behind me.

I turned. The rain was deafening. This was why I hated the bayou. You never knew where you were.

"Ronny?" I yelled. "Over here!"

No answer.

I pushed toward where I had last seen the rowboat. My foot twisted. I fell to my knees on something hard and flat, and water rushed up around my waist. I shielded my eyes, rubbed the rain from them. All around me stood the angled shapes of those crumbling bone houses.

I was in the cemetery again. That sinking city of the dead.

A laugh echoed through the storm. There was Waldo, rowing his way among the half-submerged tombs, paddling through the stone houses.

Cold rain splattered my face. My ears froze. Or were they burning hot? I couldn't tell. My lungs ached with each breath. I heard the voice again.

I heard the voice, only . . .

What I heard wasn't a single voice. It was several voices. And they weren't human.

They were howling dogs.

"No . . . no . . ." I gasped.

Something moved among the dark trees. Three,

five, eight shapes. I sloshed as fast as I could between the tombs. The muddy ground sucked my shoes off.

Now I could see the dogs. Starved animals of bone and teeth, they were so emaciated they looked almost invisible. Where the rain struck them, it outlined their shapes, moving swiftly behind the tombs.

I tried to climb to the top of one crypt, but the rain poured off the stone sides and I kept slipping. The dogs were in the open now. As one, they splashed across the mushy ground, their heads fixed on me. They held their mouths wide, teeth struck by raindrops, gleaming in the dark.

I turned and ran, frantically thrusting my way between the tombs. Then I tripped and struck my forehead on a broken stone.

Blood in my eyes, I stood up, tried to get my bearings. The dogs were moving fast.

They leaped at me.

FIFTEEN

Under the Five Trees

A sudden shriek pierced the darkness.

The dogs slid silently to a halt. I scrambled backward, falling, getting up. Heavy raindrops washed over the dogs like watercolors.

Soon there was only the splattering, empty earth around me.

I wiped the blood from my eyes and staggered to my feet. Where had the dogs gone?

Where? That's when I realized where I was.

No longer in the boneyard's alleys, I had made my way to higher ground. I stood beneath a vault of trees — five drowned oaks, crisscrossed in a half circle.

And right there amid the broken trees, with rain dripping off his smiling face, water to his knees, and his empty rowboat behind him, was Waldo.

His blind eyes glistened like black marbles.

"Ghost dogs," he said. His voice was hollow, deeper than before. "I call them on. I call them off."

I tried to step back, but only slid to my knees in the muck.

"You're nuts," I said. It felt good to say it.

"Ten years ago," Waldo said, "you were here."

My heart pounded. "What are you talking about?"

"Ten years ago, you were drowning . . . *right here,*" he said, waving his hands around as if he knew exactly where he was.

"What do you know about that?" I spat.

"I know what drowning's like," he said. His voice sounded even lower now. "Water running up your nose, filling your ears, your mouth? You panic, don't you? I know I did."

Waldo didn't even sound like the precious boy anymore. His face was changing, too. His features were sinking into themselves. His long blond hair was matted, pasted to his cheeks like dark rivulets of oil. All the color I had first seen in his face had washed away. His skin was gray.

"Your lungs burn like they're on fire," he went on, "screaming at you to fill them with air. But you don't want to breathe in water. . . ."

I glanced around, trying not to panic, looking for a way out.

"I know what it feels like," Waldo said, "because I drowned here, too. Six summers ago. The only difference is, maybe you survived. I didn't."

The storm went silent in my head.

"You were . . . one of them," I whispered.

"I *am* one of them," he said quietly. "I . . . he was playing one day and slipped into the swamp. Underwater, as he sunk, he saw the *Bellamina*, and got trapped in its railing. Then he saw a face, the captain. Soon it was me swimming to the surface. I've been here for six years, trying to figure out how I could bring my crew back. To continue the war." Waldo paused a moment, then grinned. "To *win* the war."

A thundering crash sounded in the distance. I knew right away what it was — the lock gate had fallen. Water was going to rush through the bayou. Any minute.

I heard a shrill, electric squeal. The sound system on the tour boats. A moment later, a flare shot up overhead. It blossomed red and hung in the stormy sky.

"You did this," I hissed at Waldo, as the water rose nearly to my waist. "You did something at the lock. You want to sink the tourist boats!"

"I took the blind, broken body of this boy," Waldo retorted. "I waited a long time for the *Bellamina* to rise . . . for you to return to Malpierre."

"For me?" I said. "What are —"

"I came here to find out if you knew about the first."

I shivered. The word Mrs. Cane — Abby's mother — had used. *First.*

"I don't know what you're talking about," I yelled.

"Maybe," he said quietly. "Maybe not."

A voice rippled through the darkness. "Derek!"

Waldo twisted. His head rattled from side to side, like a paint can in a mixer. "I guess I'll have to wait," he said. "Someone's coming for you. Let's give him something to do."

"Here I am!" I cried out. My voice was drowned out by the battering rain. It sounded no louder than a whisper. The distant call was moving away.

"Help!" I choked. I could hardly hear myself.

"Why are you whispering?" asked Waldo, stepping toward me. "Afraid to wake the dead? It's too late for that."

"Help . . ." My voice was hoarse with fear.

"Sorry. I've got my own helping to do," Waldo said, moving closer. "I have to bring back my crew."

"I'll stop you," I said, trying to sound strong.

"You'll try," he replied.

Waldo's dead-eyed face grinned horribly at me. I clenched my fists to punch it.

I should have been watching his hand.

By the time I saw the train, it was too late. Waldo slammed the iron toy into the side of my head so quickly that I barely heard the crack of my skull before I fell into the water.

The swamp surrounded me. Dark water filled my mouth, my nose.

The bayou wanted me.

Again.

SIXTEEN

The Hand

I tried to claw to the surface, but you can't crawl up water. The weight of it pressed on my chest like a stone.

Water of birth, water of death, alone, alone, alone . . .

The sudden words made me angry, even as I brushed them out of my mind. Would anyone save me this time?

Cold white fingers clutched at me, cold hands. Was I seeing things? It didn't matter. No one was coming. Soon I would leak away.

Shapes flew around me like smoky figures rising, falling, reaching out with long fingers. Then, a face. Black hair moving around a pale face.

Who was it?

Fingers wrapped around my hand. I tried to pull away. The grip was too strong and wouldn't let go. Cold fingers on my forehead. I struggled against them. My lungs nearly gave out. The angel ornament in my pocket suddenly seemed heavy. It weighed me down. I sank.

Then my body doubled over in the water. I broke the surface. Air! A shape huddled over me, pumping my chest, slapping my cheeks.

"Derek, Derek, Derek!"

I blew out a lungful of water. I coughed up black muck, sucked air into my mouth, coughed, breathed. I saw a face. A face I loved.

"Dad!" I cried, clutching the arms of my father. His wet face dripped on mine. "Dad!"

"Don't talk, Derek," he said. "Breathe —"

"You saved me!" I said. "Again! In the same place."

He tipped my face to the side and pumped my chest. I coughed out more black water, nearly fainting, coughing, coming to again.

"You saved me. It was you, you did it again —"

"No!" he shouted. Dad shook his head. He helped me sit up on the lid of a crypt. "No, Derek. I was there that night, ten years ago. But it wasn't me. I didn't pull you from the water. I found you, but someone else saved you."

"Who?" I asked.

He kept shaking his head. "I don't know. Here in Malpierre, ten years ago, you saw something no one else saw."

"Dad, what are you saying?"

"We'll find out together," he said, helping me up. The words made me feel hope again. "Derek, we have to find him. The first one who was translated. The dead are coming here to find him."

Hadn't Abby told me her mother said that? They were trying to find someone?

"There's one secret to understanding all this," Dad said. "And I think it's in what you saw that night. Only you know. That's why you had to come back here, to remember that night."

I was breathless. "Why didn't you ever tell me? You knew all this, and you never told me?"

He didn't answer.

I started to shake. "Your hand, Dad."

"What?"

"Show me your left hand," I said.

Ever since I'd seen pieces of a hand at the Coroner's office, pieces whose DNA matched my father's, I had hoped that whatever was left of my father's hand wasn't black and rotten like Ronny's finger.

I had hoped. But I needed proof.

"I have to see it."

He didn't move. I grabbed his wrist and forced his hand from his pocket. It was a thickly bandaged lump. Spots of dried blood, brown and dull, showed through the grimy cloth.

"Unwrap it," I said. "I have to know what it looks like. Unwrap it."

"Derek —"

Screams burst through the rain. The tourists. Sudden sirens approached from the distance. I could hear the thunder of distant helicopters approaching.

"Waldo's bringing back the *Bellamina*," I said, stumbling toward the lock, forgetting my injuries. "It's filled with dead souls. He's done this —"

Another scream broke through the storm. I recognized this one.

It was Ronny.

SEVENTEEN

Enemies

Dad and I tumbled into Waldo's empty rowboat. Rainwater in thc bottom sloshed over our feet. My arms hurt, my head hurt, but I grabbed an oar, gave Dad the other one, and together we dug into the rising floodwater. We pushed our way among the trees toward the dike.

Finally, we spotted Ronny.

He stood, soaked and silent and staring into the trees on a small spit of land. The rise barely held itself up above the water.

I noticed Dad stiffen when he saw what had become of his other son. "Ronny!" he called.

We jumped out and ran to him, still clutching our oars like weapons. Ronny didn't move.

"Where's Bonton?" I asked him.

"Gone," Ronny mumbled. "We couldn't get to the boats. Then the dogs came. He ran."

There was a rustle among the trees. A shape moved out of the branches.

I stifled a scream.

It was Abby's mother.

"She found us," said Ronny. "They all found us."

So they were here, the dead from New Orleans. I couldn't understand how they got here so quickly, but it hardly mattered. They were everywhere I was.

The dead woman's eyes moved slowly from one to the other of us, then fixed on me. Her mouth opened and that sound like metal twisting, grinding like gears being stripped, slid into my bad ear.

I sank to my knees. "Stop!"

Was she going to speak again? Was she trying to speak to me? Had she actually been to the hospital to see Abby? Her dead eyes said nothing.

Instinctively, my father moved between the woman and me. Ronny helped me to my feet and shoved me behind him.

Abby's mother took a step forward, keeping her eyes on me. The branches rustled again, and another figure appeared. Erskine Cane.

I saw then how fierce the war in the afterlife had been.

Cane and Ronny stared at each other with so much hate, it was clear that their souls had battled long and hard. Poor Virgil, stuck in Ronny's slight form, while Cane was reborn in a monster body.

But Cane and this woman were part of the Legion, and we had to try to stop them.

The woman howled something incomprehensible and ran at me. I hated fighting her, knowing that she was in the body of Abby's mother. Anger took over, and I hurled the oar at her legs. She wailed and splashed onto the ground. She twitched, stared, tried to climb to her feet.

"Leave me alone!" I yelled.

Cane charged. But Ronny was quick. He had a chunk of tombstone in his hand and threw it at Cane, catching him in the face. Cane shouted and stumbled.

Cries echoed from across the swamp.

"We have to help the tourists!" Dad yelled. The three of us took off through the trees, with Cane and the woman after us. We sloshed through the mud and up to the crest of the levee, leaving them behind.

From there, we saw the first boat. Wave after wave rushed into the waterway so quickly that the boat had no time to maneuver. In moments, its bow was submerged and began to sink. Some passengers were thrown overboard, while others scrambled frantically up the deck to the rising stern. We ran along the levee toward them until a powerful rush of water barreled past, cutting us off. We watched helplessly as their boat heaved up and over, capsizing completely. The two other boats whirled into view now, struggling to stay afloat.

"What can we do?" I yelled.

"Over here!" Ronny shouted out to the closest tourists in the water. "Swim to the levee!"

Dad was furious. He slipped into the water and clawed his way back to the top of the levee, trying to find a way to reach the people. A sudden wave rammed the second boat into the upturned hull of the first. There was a flash, and the engine exploded. Fuel sprayed across its deck to the third boat.

A scream of sound pierced my ear — or was it a scream of light? Whatever it was, I saw a gash of white in the water, and my ear stung at the same time. It sounded like iron on iron, echoing until it ended in a shriek. It was like nothing I'd ever heard before.

"The Rift has opened!" Ronny shouted.

The water churned and heaved. Something from below was pushing it out of the way — the *Bellamina*.

It rose out of the water like a dead weight thrust up from below. The water sucked at it, pulling it back down, and yet it rose, inch by inch from the depths. A second explosion from the tour boats spilled burning fuel onto its drenched old decks.

The *Bellamina* was a great, horrible shape, black as night, dripping with smoking moss and burning vines and rotten weeds. Water poured off its sagging decks. It seemed ready to crumble in on itself, and yet it rose higher. Its broken, spokeless side-wheels turned and squealed, glistening in the battering rain. Soon the old boat was all we could see. It dwarfed the tiny tour boats.

Dark shapes moved against the sagging rails, from one deck to the next, all the way up to the peak. The rain dripped, crosshatching them, giving them shape, size, bulk.

"The dead souls of the smugglers," Ronny said under his breath.

Standing on top of the broken lock gate was the precious boy himself, Waldo, watching the scene he had made happen. His voice rose into a terrible bellow. "Boys, come and get 'em!"

Without pause, the shapes leaped from the *Bellamina*'s decks and dived at the tourists.

EIGHTEEN

The Old Black Boat

Ronny exploded in anger. "No, no, no!" Then he jumped off the levee, into the water.

"Ronny!" yelled Dad. "Get back here —"

But Ronny powered through the waves and reached the rising steamboat in moments. Grabbing a spoke of the side-wheel, he hoisted himself aboard. Then Dad jumped in too, swam underwater to the boat, and clambered onto the main deck.

I couldn't go in that water. I couldn't.

I watched as the last of the dead souls plunged into the churning waves. At first there was gargling, yelling, splashing, confusion. Then it was over.

The tourists rose from the depths.

Their faces gleamed in the firelight, gray, emotionless. The pastel-dressed women, the chubby bearded men, were now possessed by the dead. Their gray fingers clutched at the *Bellamina*'s hull. As they pulled themselves up on deck, one after another, I realized what I hadn't before. The translated dead weren't human anymore. The rushing water didn't stop them — it didn't even slow them down. They gripped the sides of the steamboat with powerful arms. Being dead had given them strength beyond normal strength.

As one, the dead vanished inside the cabins. The sound of cracking and splintering wood echoed across the water. Then they were back, wielding pistols and cutlasses.

The army was armed.

Ronny and Dad were aboard now, swinging iron pipes like baseball bats. Three translated souls fell quickly before them. But in moments, they crawled to their feet again. The dead were back up.

I couldn't watch anymore. I found myself neck-deep in the water, my arms flailing wildly toward the *Bellamina*. I felt her oily, slick, scummy, rotten planks and I pulled myself onto the deck.

"I hoped it wasn't true!" a voice said behind me. I turned, expecting the worst.

Bonton hobbled toward me, his eyes on fire. "I didn't want to believe it. Waldo is their captain. *My* precious boy! I have to try to stop him. . . ." He tore a piece of railing from a rotten stairway and stormed off, shouting at the top of his lungs. His false foot didn't stop him, just as age hadn't stopped Bob Lemon.

"Wait!" I cried. I spotted a cutlass on the floor and grabbed it. I wasn't sure if anything could stop the dead, but I had to try. Bonton and I moved together toward the main hall of the ship, where Ronny and Dad were.

A whistle sliced through the air. We turned. The bayou dogs stood panting on the deck behind us, heads low, teeth bared. Waldo stood behind them.

His small face twisted in anger. "You simple old man!" he crowed at Bonton, his voice even deeper than before. "Did you really think I was your son — all these years?"

Bonton was torn with rage and sorrow. "You —"

Before he could finish, Waldo whistled again and the dogs rippled across the air, skeletal beasts. Bonton screamed. I was there fast, chopping the air with the old sword. The dogs, untranslated, as immaterial as ghosts, leaped right through my blade.

"You little creep!" I shouted at Waldo.

Waldo laughed, then rushed at us. I held the old sword steady, but Waldo lunged low and arched up with his bony arms. My cutlass swung wildly to the side, struck the wall, snapped, and fell to the floor. Bonton grabbed the boy and pulled him off me.

Saber bloodied, saber broken, saber buried, burned, reborn . . .

Waldo scrambled to his feet as I jabbed out with the broken sword. At the same time, Bonton threw himself between us.

"No!" I cried.

Bonton screamed. He dropped his wooden stake and staggered from the room. My blade had struck him.

Insane with anger, I turned back to Waldo, but he darted away. "Don't worry, we'll meet again, mystery boy!" he snarled. The dogs bounded out of sight behind him.

Mystery boy? I had no time to wonder what he meant, because Ronny stumbled into the hall. In one hand was his length of iron piping. A swatch of ragged wet cloth dangled from it. In the other hand, he held an old flintlock pistol by its barrel.

"Above you —" he cried.

One of the smugglers, now in cargo shorts and sneakers, leaped down from the gallery above the main hall. My shoulder blade stung with sudden pain. I dropped to my knees.

The dead man arched for a second blow, but Ronny swung the pipe like a machine. The guy's arm flew across the room. There was a howl — not of pain, but of anger. Ronny fought the creature away from me. I wanted to cry out, but there was no time. We couldn't stop fighting.

Two more dead men appeared. One still had a camera dangling from his neck. They rushed at me. I slipped on the mucky deck and fell against the wall. It cracked into splinters, and I tumbled onto a set of stairs, losing the broken saber. The stairs burst their boards, and I dropped hard into a room on a lower deck.

"Ronny!" I shouted. But then a tourist — a teenager not quite as old as Ronny — was thrown down next to me by one of the gray-faced men.

"What's happening?" the boy asked me.

I knew what was happening. The dead needed drowning victims to translate into.

"We have to get off this boat!" I said.

The dead man lingered at the top of the stairs for a moment, saw me, turned, and walked away. Why?

I didn't have to wait long for the answer.

"What's hap —" the boy started again. A shape rose from the submerged far side of the room, dripping water from invisible shoulders.

"Get out of here!" I yelled to the boy. "Run. Run!" I tried to push him toward the broken stairs, but we both slipped and splashed into the water again. I knew what the shape wanted.

"Get out —"

I pulled the boy to his feet and shoved him toward a small door behind us. My foot dragged on the floor, caught the doorframe, and I tripped. The door slammed shut, trapping us both inside the room. Water was up to our waists.

The shape made no noise, moving unstoppably toward us.

The boy grabbed my arm, not understanding.

The thing lunged at us.

NINETEEN

The Meaning of Dreams

But not at me.

No.

The shape twisted in midair with the speed of lightning. It leaped at the terrified boy. I grabbed for him, missed. The soul and the boy disappeared underwater.

I knew what came next.

The water churned, bubbled, calmed. I knew it would. I had seen it before.

I knew what came next. Is that what Dad meant?

Had I seen a translation before?

I dug my feet into the floor, moved quickly along the wall, and made my way to the door on the far side of the room. Pausing for breath, I looked back. The boy rose out of the water. For an instant my heart broke. His eyes were dead, his skin without color. He sloshed toward me, a new foot soldier for the Legion.

I pushed through the door and scrambled up to the

main deck. Ronny and Dad were standing there together, exhausted, angry, horrified, but ready for more. The battle wasn't over.

Erskine Cane moved his hulking, gray-faced bulk onto the main deck. Behind him were the original dead from the Bordelon crash. His wife. The one-armed conductor. The gray-haired man. Twitchy. The others.

And forty new ones.

Their voices in my ear were deafening, but over it all I heard a scratchy laugh. The Legion parted. Waldo stood there, laughing like a mad, old soul.

"Derek Stone," he began. "Have you discovered —"

"Shut up!" I cried. I didn't want to hear his voice a second longer. Tearing the wooden angel out of my pocket, I ran at Waldo. My legs — chunky, worn out, bruised beyond belief — carried me past the dead. I was on him in seconds.

I smashed the angel into his face with all my strength. He shrieked. The angel shattered in my hands. Waldo fell to his knees, groaning, while something clanked and splashed to the deck at my feet.

It was a rusty iron key. I snatched it up.

Seeing it in my hand, Waldo exploded in anger.

And the dead swarmed.

TWENTY

On the Move

The dead didn't get far. With a roar, Bonton's airboat whumped over the capsized tour boats and thudded onto the *Bellamina*'s deck. It crashed through the sodden rails and into the main hall, propeller spinning wildly.

"Don't you dead ones come any closer!" Bonton shouted from the pilot's seat. With a swift turn of the wheel, he lurched the boat around so that the blades were flashing like a giant open fan between us and the dead. "Unless you want to be sliced to bits and fried up for supper!"

Still bleeding from his forehead, Bonton also clutched a giant flare gun.

Waldo let out a cry like a strangled wolf. His eyes bulged as he stared, frozen, at the rusted key in my hand. He wanted it.

The Legion waited.

My heart leaped into my throat. It was a standoff — the four of us against an army of the dead. We could do little against them, but they couldn't move any closer.

The propeller's blades whirred madly.

Cane grunted. The Legion turned. I guessed they had gotten what they came for — more bodies. They didn't get me. But there was always the next time. Now nearly fifty strong, they piled off the deck and onto the soaked ground, where the floodwater had leveled out.

As the airboat's propellers spun, we watched them disappear into the night. Before they vanished, Waldo whistled. The ghostly dogs raced through the trees, to his side.

The voices ebbed in my ear, but sirens crisscrossed one another, moving toward us. The *thuck-thuck* of helicopters battered the air overhead.

The police — and whoever else — had arrived.

Dad grabbed my shoulders. "You have to keep moving," he said. "No matter what happens, remember that I love you, even if you don't see me for a while —"

"Dad, no!" I said. "This is crazy. You're *not* going away again —"

He stared at the key in my hand. The handle was a scalloped oval with a flower shape inside. The teeth at the end of the barrel were oddly notched. It was old.

"What is this?" I asked him. "What does it open?"

Dad released his grip on me and pulled away slowly. "I don't know. But we can't let the police find us together," he said. "To stop the Legion we need to split up, here and now. I'll find you again, I promise. Right now, I'll distract the police. Get out of here —"

"Dad, please, no! You can't be a hit-and-run dad! You can't go. You have to —"

"You need to be free!" he shouted, turning to shore. "This war has been going on for a long time, and we're in the middle of it now. We might also be there at the end of it, if we do what we can. If *you* do what *you* can, Derek." He jumped into the water, waded to land, and stomped off in the rain. He began to run loudly through the trees, drawing the gleam of searchlights after him.

"*If* I *do what* I *can?*" I muttered. "All I can do is run."

That's when Bonton fell out of the pilot's seat.

"Bonton!" cried Ronny. We ran to him. The man's eyes were silvery. He moaned, lifting his hands to the great gash on the side of his head.

TWENTY-ONE

Staying Alive

We carried Bonton to the top of the levee and set him down. I thought of how we'd left Bob Lemon in the dark house. It seemed so long ago. There were fewer of us every minute.

I tried to prop his head up, but Bonton waved me away. "You helped me enough, Derek," he said. "You kept the dead away from me. I'll go natural. That's a blessing. It's okay for me now. I'll go soon."

"No —" I said.

Grimacing, he shook his head. "That night years ago, Derek, I heard the dogs, but came too late to save you. Someone already had. Stuffed in your pocket, dry as can be, was this." He dug his hand in the lining of his prosthetic boot and slid out a plastic bag with a folded yellow envelope inside. "Maybe you'll know what it means."

Bonton made a noise then. His face twisted in pain, then eased slowly, the lines and creases fading away.

He was gone.

Trembling, I opened the envelope. Inside was a wrinkled photograph. I knew from the train books in my father's collection that it was an early photograph, from around 1850 or so, before the Civil War. The image was small, but detailed and clear.

It was a plantation house. A huge old mansion with columns across the front, a deep porch, and a gallery across the second floor with a wrought-iron railing. Ivy covered one side of the house, and wisps of Spanish moss hung down over an iron fence in the foreground.

The scrollwork in the fence was flower-shaped, the same as on the handle of the iron key.

All of the details in the photograph were various shades of brown, but the house itself was hand-colored with a crimson wash. I remembered what Abby had told me on the phone earlier that day.

"The red house," I blurted out.

"What?" asked Ronny, glancing at the photograph.

"The red house," I repeated, looking at the key and wondering why it had been hidden in my house. "Abby told me the dead are heading there. They're looking for someone or something."

I heard more sirens and shouts pulling away from us on the other side of the swamp. Dad was leading the police on a chase. Maybe he'd escape. Maybe he'd get caught. I didn't know. I hadn't seen his hand, so I wasn't sure who or what he even was now, but he was helping us stay free.

Ronny pulled me to my feet. "The police will find Bonton and take care of him," he said, scanning the receding water. "Maybe they'll even piece together what happened here. They'll find another explanation for it. *Any* other explanation. But they're part of it now. It's getting bigger. We have to keep moving."

So. It was Ronny and me. Alone again.

But maybe there was someone else to think about, too.

I made one final call on my cell before the battery died completely. Before I got three words out, Abby cut me off.

"Meet me at the train station in Baton Rouge," she said. "Tomorrow at noon. I know where the red house is."

My heart skipped. "Tell me. I'm ready for anything."

"Not for this," she said, her voice faltering. "Meet me at the station. I have to tell you in person. There's something you don't —"

The phone went dead.

I turned to Ronny. "We're going to Baton Rouge."

He searched my face. "Why?" he asked. "To do what?"

I opened my mouth, but closed it again. I had no answer. Not that Ronny, for all his questions, seemed to expect one. He knew that no matter what we might imagine, the answers would be more terrifying than we could possibly believe. But we needed to know the truth, no matter how awful.

The water roared before us, and the giant black steamboat tilted, throwing waves up all around it. It had released its centuries-old dead. It was done. Slowly it leaned, sank into the black floodwater, and was gone at last.

Ronny looked straight up through the trees at the night sky. "More rain coming."

"You sound like Waldo," I said — then regretted it.

"I *am* like Waldo," he snapped, tapping his chest with his blackened finger. "And more rain *is* coming, so be ready. Night isn't over yet. We'd better move. I won't be here forever."

Making sure the old key was safely in my pocket, I followed Ronny to Waldo's rowboat. We climbed in and let it drift past the cemetery, the vault of trees, the shack, everything, until we reached Samantha's car. It was more mangled from Ronny's driving than I remembered. Maybe if Sam knew what was going on, she'd want us to keep the car as long as we needed it. When it wouldn't run anymore, she'd want us to find another and another, just to keep the horror away as long as possible.

Any sane person would.

Ronny started the car, and an hour later we were out of the bayous, heading north to Baton Rouge.

So this is life now. Home is gone. Family is gone. The army of the dead is growing, making their way across the land. Normal doesn't exist for me anymore.

Soon it won't exist for anyone else, either.

The old way of life is over.

This is war.

Don't miss the next volume in Derek's story . . .

The Red House

Turn the page for a special sneak peek!

The Red House

"He died."

Two words, and my dumb little life changed forever.

Six letters, and the world I believed in vanished into nothing, like fog.

"I won't believe it!" I cried, falling to my knees. "I won't!"

"You must believe it," was the stone cold reply.

As sunny and warm as the day began, night dropped hard and fast like the lid of a coffin.

The horror of it made me sick. I didn't want to go on. I *couldn't* go on.

I mean, how would *you* feel if someone told you —

Wait.

You couldn't possibly know how you'd feel unless you understood — really understood — what I'm talking about.

So let me wipe the blood from my forehead and go back nine hours to this morning.

I'll tell you everything that happened from that moment to now. You need to know where we came from, to understand where we are now.

We? Right. Let me start there.

My name is Derek Stone. I'm fourteen, fat, smarter than most people I know, and on the run. Nine hours ago, my older brother, Ronny, and I were holed up in a filthy room in a fleabag hotel on the outskirts of Baton Rouge, Louisiana. We'd been there since four a.m. the night before.

I opened my eyes. It was 11:21 a.m. The blinds were down, but sunlight sliced through them like a hot knife through butter. The air was a white haze. The room was an oven.

"How'd you pick this dump, anyway?" I asked Ronny, rolling off the mattress and onto my feet. "I feel horrible."

"You look horrible," Ronny snorted from the bathroom sink. "Being on the run means being on a budget. Our money's almost out."

I flipped open my cell. Black screen. Dead battery.

"I wish I could charge this thing," I said. "In case Abby calls again."

Abby Donner. My phone had died last night in the middle of a call from her.

More on her later.

"Dump that thing," said Ronny. "The cops can trace it, right? Besides, Abby's train comes in half an hour. Get dressed."

I pulled on my pants and shirt and muscled Ronny out of the bathroom. I held my breath as he passed.

Why did I hold my breath? Because Ronny is decaying.

"Decaying?" you say. "The dude's only nineteen. How could he be decaying? Only corpses do that, right?"

Right. Only corpses.

Man, I'm tired of telling this story. But you need to hear it. Your life depends on it, though you may not know it yet. So listen up, and bear with me. There's a lot to tell, and not much time.

A few weeks ago Ronny, my father, and I were in a bad train wreck. Maybe you heard about it. Big news. The old bridge over Bordelon Gap collapsed. Our train fell into the ravine. Ronny was one of nine passengers killed.

Then he came back.

Came back?

Trust me, that's the easy part.

"We're out of here," Ronny said. He pulled me into the hotel hallway with all my worldly possessions: twenty-something dollars, twenty pounds of extra fat, a headache, and a case of the shakes.

"Let's skidaddle," he added.

Skidaddle? That's exactly what I'm talking about.

Ronny came back from the train wreck — at least, his body did. Inside him was the soul of a young man named Virgil Black. Virgil died in an almost identical train crash at the same place back in 1938. Because the two accidents were so alike, and because the curtain that separates the worlds of the living and the dead has been torn — I call it the *Rift* — souls in the afterlife were able to enter the crash victims at the moment they died.

"*Enter* the crash victims?" you say.

Yep. Reanimate them.

Like, "Hello! We're back!"

It's the old body, but a different soul. I call this grotesque soul-switching *translation*.

Another one of the train wreck victims was my father. He was missing for weeks, presumed dead, since all they could find of him was his finger. But then he turned up alive and *un*translated . . . I think.

The souls who came back are a pack of notorious convicts, led by a murderous thug called Erskine Cane. I'd learned pretty quickly that these dark souls are only the advance troops of a huge, massive dead-guy army called the Legion.

The Legion.

The word makes me nauseous.

"Come on," Ronny said, slinging his small bag into the trunk of a beat-up green Subaru that belonged to his ex-girlfriend, Samantha. It had looked much nicer before we'd borrowed it. "Clock's ticking." I slid into the passenger seat.

According to Ronny — er, Virgil — for centuries, the evil souls of the Legion have been warring against good souls in the afterlife. And they're winning. Once they discovered the Rift, they began translating into dead bodies and bringing their war up here.

Why?

To take over.

"I don't like this," Ronny said. He slowed the car and pulled over to the curb to let four police cruisers tear past us.

"You don't think they know about us, do you?" I said.

"Maybe," he said quietly. "Maybe Uncle Carl told them to look for us." The police cars roared up the street and away. After a minute, Ronny pulled back into traffic.

My father's brother Carl had stayed with me in New Orleans after the train crash. He was there when Ronny came back, but he didn't know the whole story. He just thought Ronny was out of sorts, traumatized. He couldn't have imagined the truth. Uncle Carl was out of town when Erskine Cane burned down our house in the French Quarter.

Ronny and I had been hiding out ever since. It was only a matter of time before the cops got involved, really. With a mass translation in the bayou, with Dad leading the cops on a wild goose chase so we could get away, with people "dying" and then mysteriously "coming back," the cops would soon be all over our war with the dead.

The war, I called it.

Simple, but effective.

"I'll park a few blocks from the station, just to be safe," Ronny said. Then he snorted. "Safe? Some joke, huh?"

Neither one of us was laughing.

"Here we are." Ronny stopped the Subaru at a curb three and a half blocks from the train station. "Hurry it up, Tubs."

There's love for you. One of the weirdest things about Ronny is that even though he's Virgil Black now — a farm boy from upstate in Shongaloo — there are still bits of Ronny in him. An occasional look. A phrase. A gesture. Something.

So I still call him Ronny.

Virgil doesn't seem to mind.

I followed him along the sidewalk. It was 11:51 a.m. Our day had begun.

Abby's train was due at noon, and it was four minutes to twelve by the time we arrived in the main concourse of the train station.

Almost the first thing I saw was the blazer.

Navy blue, shiny, saggy in the shoulders, with a bulge under the left arm. And then another blazer just like it, and another, and another. Between and above the baggy shoulders were thick necks, sweaty foreheads, and darting eyes.

"Police?" I said. "Federal agents?"

Ronny glanced furiously from face to face as the men moved quickly into every corner of the large room. "This is bad. If they bring us in, they won't believe a word we say, and the Legion will keep growing until it's too late. Slip into the shadows. If I lose you, I'll meet you on the street behind the building. Keep out of sight. We may have to start running."

Running? That loosened something in my head, and strange words echoed from my memory.

Children of light, lost, so lost, running in darkness . . .

I shivered to hear those words in my mind. Like other words I'd "heard" since the accident, I had no clue what these meant. But they sure seemed to be about Ronny and me.

. . . lost, so lost, running in darkness . . .

And maybe Abby, too.

Ronny pulled me out of the main room, toward platform 13. We ducked into a bagel shop when a couple of guys in blazers passed.

"Uh-oh, Ronny," I whispered. "Look up there."

A flat-screen TV behind the counter showed grainy nighttime footage of water rushing through a bayou.

Malpierre. I knew it.

My chest buzzed when a TV voiceover began describing the incident. I couldn't hear everything, but I could hear enough. "Flash flood . . . broken lock . . . crested levees . . . bayou tour boats . . . startling rescue . . ." The video then showed a car hidden among the bayou overgrowth.

Our green Subaru.

"That's it," Ronny said. "They must have spotted the car outside. They're closing in. There's her train."

The train from New Orleans squealed to a stop, and right away, the platform was flooded with passengers. We waited in the bagel shop, scanning the crowd. Almost the last person to leave the train was a girl with long brown hair tied in a loose ponytail. Abby Donner. She wore blue shorts and a green T-shirt, and had a big handbag slung over her shoulder.

Abby had broken her ankle in the train wreck a month ago, but when she walked down the platform, I saw that her ankle cast was gone. She was using a wooden cane.

"I'm going," I said.

"Wait for her to come a little closer —" Ronny grabbed my arm.

"I'm going." I pushed out of the shop and walked quickly to the platform, head down, hoping no one would notice me.

Abby's eyes were tired, and her face looked pale, but she managed a smile when she spotted me. "Hey, Derek."

"We can't be here," I whispered, taking her arm.

"Hello to you, too," she said, stopping. "Do you even know what I went through to track down that weird old house for you?"

"Do you even know how many cops are in the station right now, waiting to nab us?" I whispered.

Her face changed. Narrowing her eyes, she scanned the concourse. "Whoa. Okay, head for the west exit. It's closest. Believe me, I scoped it out. I had all kinds of maps and diagrams and I used MapQuest and —"

"Just come on," I said, and we hurried down the platform.

Some army, huh?

A fat boy, his dead brother, and a chatty girl with a cane.

We didn't stand a chance.

All at once, someone in a blue blazer bolted across the concourse toward our platform. A shrill whistle sounded, a man yelled, and agents fanned out across the big room. I glanced over at the bagel shop. Ronny was gone.

OLIVER NOCTURNE

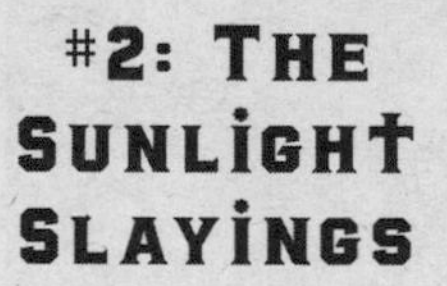

Oliver is convinced that he's lost the only real friends he's ever had—Emalie and Dean. But then Dean turns up, still dead but now a zombie, and apparently he isn't holding any grudges. Who brought Dean back—and why? And what is going on with Emalie—could she be behind the magical slayings of several young vampires? Oliver and Dean must discover the truth before Oliver himself winds up turned to dust.